The Case of

Dragon Feast

Book 3 in the Barry Hargrove Mysteries

by

Bob Nailor

This page left blank

ISBN: 978-1-61877-175-9

The Case of Dragon Feast

Discover other titles by Bob Nailor at:
www.bobnailor.com

Cover collage by Bob Nailor

Dedication

This book is dedicated to Denise Vitola, author of the "Ty Merrick" series. She is my writing mentor, my dear friend, and unknowingly, sometimes, my Muse

This page left blank

Table of Contents

CHAPTER ONE

The Case

"The dragon ate her."

His words were blunt, succinct, and spoken with absolutely no sense or hint of humor.

I observed him, waiting for any crack in that sincere, twenty-something year old face. Nothing. I glanced at the clock; almost 5 p.m. and my stomach was screaming to be fed.

Bang!

I listened to the firework scream toward its zenith.

Pop! Crackle! Sizzle!

I shook my head. Tomorrow would be Lantern Festival. Sure. Why wouldn't somebody start today? I shook my head knowing it would be a night of sporadic fireworks.

I remembered how this whole scene began. I was working on my newspaper crossword. I scowled remembering my word choice - 22 down, desire. I had the word 'like' written and now on 27 across, 5 letters starting with 'I' for 'open soda' didn't make sense. I was staring at my word choices when my office door opened. My stomach had growled, and a young man stood hesitantly, deciding whether to enter or not.

I opened my top desk drawer and slid the folded newspaper into it. Smiling, I motioned for the young man to come forward as I stood.

"Welcome," I said. "The name is Barry Hargrove." I extended my hand to shake.

"You're the detective," he said and moved across the office toward me, all the while scanning the room with a certain disdain.

I glanced about my office. Stark. Sterile. A desk with a lamp, my chair, two chairs on the other side, a file cabinet, a small table to the side with a coffee maker, a small refrigerator, a microwave, and three ill-chosen framed pictures on the walls. Oof-white walls and cement gray heavy-duty carpeting added nothing to the ambiance.

"I'm James Zimmer." He stretched out his hand to shake mine.

"So, Mr. Zimmer, exactly what brings you to seek my services?"

I shook his hand; he had a firm grip. "Have a seat." I motioned to the two chairs in front of my desk as I sat.

"Mr. Hargrove..." he started, also sitting.

"Detective Hargrove, please," I corrected with a shrug.

"My girlfriend is missing and I was told you really know your stuff."

I smiled. "Not sure who told you that, but I like to think I can do the job." I leaned over my desk. "How long has she been missing? Did you go to the police? Are you sure she isn't visiting her parents, or avoiding you?"

Zimmer twisted his lips in a sneer. "First, my girlfriend has no parents. They were killed when she was eleven, and she was raised in several foster homes." He shrugged. "She really never had anyone she would call parents. Second, of course I went to the police. They've spent some time on the case but have come up with nothing. It was there I heard your name being bandied about."

I attempted not to react to his last words. I was sure my buddy and ex-partner, Leroy Williamson, would know something. A visit to the precinct was obvious if I took the job for this young man before me.

"Who did you work with at the police station?" I asked.

"Detective Jim Preston." Once again, he shrugged. "He didn't really seem to care about whether he found Holly or not." A grin turned the edges of lips. "When I told him a dragon ate her, well, he snapped the lead on his pencil, cocked an eye toward me, and took a deep breath."

And, this is where we were. I attempted to discern any Tom foolery in him. Still, his expression remained stoic.

I hesitated, but still had to ask. "A dragon ate her?"

Zimmer nodded. "A purple one as I was told. We were here in Chinatown for the celebration of Chinese New Year and she asked me to get something to eat. I left her and when I returned, she was gone. When I asked those standing nearby, they all told me the same thing. The dragon ate her." He sat in the chair, hands clasped, rolling his thumbs around each other. "Yeah, Detective Preston was nice, but I think he thought I was crazy. He told me he'd look into it and let me know."

"You want me to find her, right?" I asked.

"If you would. How much?"

I told him my fees and how it worked. He cringed.

"I'm a college student, detective. I have a little savings that I was going to use for Holly and I to go to Fiji during the summer, but..." His voice trailed away. After a deep sigh he gazed at me. "Of course, no Holly, no vacation. Plus, I'd rather have Holly than a vacation."

Watching him, I could see the anguish, the internal fight over a decision.

"Fine, Detective Hargrove. I'll hire you. May I bring you a check tomorrow morning?"

"That would be fine," I replied and glanced at the clock - five fifteen. I was sure Willie would be headed home to his family and a delicious evening meal. Tomorrow, I thought. Willie will be pleased to see me, I'm sure. I grinned at the irony. If anything, I was the last person he wanted to see.

"Is there something funny?" Zimmer asked, scowling at me.

"No," I replied. "I plan to go to the precinct tomorrow morning and my ex-partner who happens to work Missing Persons will be less than pleased to see my mug so early."

Zimmer nodded. "What else do you need to know."

I took out my notebook. "We have a few standard questions. Your girlfriend's full name?"

"Holly Brockwood."

"Do you have a picture of her I could have?"

Zimmer reached into his hip pocket and pulled out his wallet.

"Here's one of us at the park. Will it be okay?"

I glanced at the picture - a little hazy, but I would be able to recognize Holly if I found her.

"It's fine. May I keep this?"

He nodded approval and I placed it to the side.

"Now, her address?"

"She lives on campus in the Kappa Kappa Gamma house."

"Do you know where she is from... what she calls home?"

"Someplace near Toledo, Ohio. I think the town name starts with a 'D' like 'Def' or "Del' - I'm not sure."

"How old is she?"

"Same as me, twenty."

I grinned. "So, I could assume she wouldn't be out bar hopping."

Zimmer's face paled. "No. She is very religious and doesn't drink or smoke." He paused. "And, no, we don't do drugs, either." A slight hint of pink colored his cheeks. "Neither of us have had sex, in case you need to know that. We're both virgins and want to be so when we marry."

Without thinking, I nodded, yet, my mind flashed with the idea, if nothing else, that particular point could be in her favor as a deterrent. "Can you tell me a little about how she disappeared? I mean, beyond the dragon ate her." I decided there was no reason to upset the young man with the possibility currently running rampant in my mind.

"From what I could tell when I was talking with the bystanders, the dragon head was the largest they'd ever seen, and the body was larger, covering the dancers. As the one old man said, it was like the dancing lion, but bigger, and a dragon."

Again, I nodded.

"Oh, they said the dragon licked her face with its tongue, then lifted up, opened its mouth, and engulfed her. She was inside the dragon's mouth and disappeared."

I tried to envision the size of the dragon head that could hold a person as described and the men - it had to be men - who could manipulate her into the dragon.

"They said," Zimmer continued. "She probably would be passed from person to person and then released on down the street."

Again, he paused. "I walked the street. I waited in the car hoping Holly would show up. She didn't." He sighed. "I waited two hours after the festivities ended." He shook his head. "I went to the police the next day. They told me to wait three days. So, I did and then talked to Preston." Again, he sighed.

"That was over two weeks ago. Nothing."

"Fine," I said. "You can bring me the check tomorrow. I'll take the case. Meet me here about eleven; I should be back from the precinct by then."

I watched him, unsure if he was in or out.

"I'll be here and if you're not, I'll wait," Zimmer said.

We shook hands and he left.

I watched him exit the door; my stomach growled. I knew I had to get to Chang's restaurant and hoped Bingwen had improved on making his father's specialty - khorkhog, assuming there'd be any left at this hour.

Not wanting to waste any more time, I grabbed my notepad and the picture of Holly. Once more my stomach growled. I couldn't wait to walk through those big red doors with the matching golden dragons. I grinned. How appropriate, I thought.

CHAPTER TWO

More Data

I ambled into Chang's and was immediately greeted with a smile by the waitress, Mei and a completely new atmosphere.

"You late tonight," she said. "You want regular seat?"

I nodded absently and she led me to my favorite table back in a corner where I could watch the other patrons and not be bothered. The place wasn't too busy, so I was able to do a quick survey; nobody caught my attention. But what did catch my attention was the new decor. Bingwen had changed things around with new tables and chairs. The walls no longer had various Chinese motifs, but were polished teakwood. I immediately noticed the new bar with its LED lighting which hadn't been there on my last visit two days earlier.

Mei stood quietly at the booth as I sat down. She smiled.

"You want khorkhog, Jasmine tea, egg roll and..." She left the sentence unfinished.

"Make it two egg rolls and when you bring me the meal, make sure to include a bowl of the juices so I can dip the meat and veggies."

Mei nodded, disappeared, and quickly reappeared with a pot of Jasmine tea and two cups which she placed on the black lacquer and gold trimmed table.

I raised an eyebrow.

"Mr. Chang say he come join." Her face paled. "It okay I tell him you here?"

"That's fine, Mei," I replied. "I can spend a little time talking to Bing... uh, Mr. Chang." I pulled the picture out of Holly and placed it on the table.

Mei glanced at the picture, turned and walked away.

I poured a cup of tea and began to sip when Bingwen appeared from the back.

"Sorry, I didn't meet you at the door," he said, slipping into the booth. "I was making sure there was enough khorkhog.' He grinned. "Just in case you decided to come in for supper." He shrugged. "I try to keep at least one serving back until the last of the evening." He winked. "Favorite customer."

"I appreciate that, Bing," I replied and then waved my hand to encompass the new restaurant interior. "What gives?"

Bingwen grinned. "I no longer wish to have father's restaurant. This my restaurant, now." He gazed about. "You like?"

"Very nice," I replied and filled his teacup with Jasmine tea.

I picked up the picture of Holly. "Do you recognize her?"

Bing took the picture and gave it a good scrutinizing before handing it back. He shook his head. "Never seen her. Why?"

"A dragon licked and then ate her." I waited for Bing to stop laughing.

"A dragon ate her? If that is true, what you are looking for won't look like that." He pointed at the picture.

"It was during Chinese New Year festival." I tried not to grin too much. "Seems while her boyfriend was getting them something to eat, one of the..."

Suddenly, I realized the problem.

"He said a dragon licked her, lifted up, and then swallowed her." I sat there shaking my head. "Most dragons are carried aloft on poles above the people. This sounds more like a dancing lion, but..." My mind raced; my eyes widened.

"What is it?" Bingwen asked.

"When my client was telling me about the event, I tried to visualize the size of the dragon's head. I'd totally forgotten about the fact the dragon is held aloft. I'm thinking this was more like a lion, but that usually only involves two people." I pondered, letting my thoughts roll through my mind.

"Dancing Lions are only two people," Bingwen agreed while pouring himself another cup of tea.

Glancing up, he noticed three people walk in the front doors.

"I'll be right back," he whispered, stood, and moved to greet the customers with a slight bow. He was on his way back to my booth when a gentleman in an off-white linen suit strolled in. There was an air about the new person. Bingwen stopped dead in his tracks, turned, and bowed ever so politely to him. He motioned to a booth off in a distant corner. The man offered a casual glance at the patrons, nodded and followed Bingwen.

Bingwen walked into the kitchen, there was some yelling in Chinese, and a waitress exploded through the doors and hustled toward the man in the linen suit.

I kept a low profile, but I was curious and waited for Bingwen to return. He did.

Nodding toward the back corner where the newest customer sat, I asked, "Who is he?"

"That is Fai Yue. He now leader of Blue Lotus Society." I could see Bingwen shiver as a chill coursed his body. "Very powerful."

I nodded, remembering how Bingwen's father had died and the Blue Lotus Society was involved.

Mei appeared with the egg rolls. She glanced again at the picture.

"Do you know her?" I asked.

"No. She pretty." Mei appraised me. "You girlfriend? Daughter?"

I shook my head and grinned. "No. She is my current search. Her boyfriend says she disappeared during the Chinese New Year festival."

Mei's eyebrows furrowed, creating a slight crease in the forehead.

"How she disappear?"

I gazed up at her innocent look, yet sincere concern.

"She was eaten by a dragon," I said, waiting to see the response.

Again, her eyebrows furrowed in thought. "A dragon ate her?"

"That's the story I was told, Mei," I replied. "Her boyfriend went to get them something to eat and when he returned, she was gone. He asked about her to the crowd nearby, they all claimed the dragon ate her."

Mei frowned. "Dragon no eat people."

I leaned back in the booth. "Well, according to everyone at the parade, this one did."

"How? Dragon float in sky."

"That is my dilemma, Mei. If they'd said a lion ate her, it would make more sense."

"My cousin, Lian Yoon, he one of many for the Lucky Green Dragon. Maybe he know?"

Bingwen eased back in the booth, sipping his tea, all the while keeping an eye on Fai Yue.

"Mei, the new customers at table nineteen will need help." He lifted his cup of tea.

She bowed and scurried across the restaurant to the latest customers.

"Sorry," I said. "She was helping me with my latest case. It was my fault she wasn't working. She needs to connect me with her cousin, Lian Yoon."

Bingwen sighed and shook his head. "He..."

I watched my host struggle with the words, frowning and grimacing.

"Lian is difficult to find," Bingwen finally said. "He seems to float from job to job." Bingwen grimaced. "He always has money; a lot of it and I don't know where he can earn that much working odd jobs at restaurants and such."

"So, you know Lian?"

Bingwen nodded. "He worked for me..." He closed his eyes in thought. "He worked about three days... okay, he showed up three days and spent most of it shuffling around doing nothing and keeping busy doing that. He spent a lot of time out back." My host grinned. "He seemed to enjoy taking out the garbage so he could be outside."

"You mean, after three days, he decided to move on?" I was intrigued.

Once more Bingwen gave a slight frown. "It was a mutual agreement. I was going to fire him; so, he quit."

Mei appeared with my meal. The khorkhog smelled great. I tasted it, my eyes widening in surprise. Mei disappeared before I could talk to her.

"You seem to have mastered your father's technique. This reminds me of how he made it."

Bingwen smiled and nodded happily. "So glad you like it."

"Do you have an address for Lian? Some place I can maybe find him?"

"The address I have is almost three years old." He shrugged. "He might still live there, but trying to catch him at home will be difficult."

"Maybe I should have Mei help me?" I countered.

"She gets off a little after nine tonight..."

Mei came out the kitchen doors with tea for the new customers.

"Mei!" Bingwen called. "When you finish, come here."

She nodded and again scurried to deliver the tea to the table. I watched her as she approached my table, her eyes filled with questions.

"You need something?" she asked Bingwen.

"It's me, Mei, not him," I said. "You said your cousin helps with the dragon. Could you introduce me to him? Maybe he has some insight to my problem."

Mei glanced at Bingwen.

"I told him you are available after nine tonight — if you wish."

"Yes, I will help," Mei whispered. "Tonight."

"Xièxiè, (thank you)" I replied.

Mei smiled and then disappeared into the kitchen.

"Do you think Lian will know about the eating dragon?" Bingwen asked.

I dipped a carrot into the brown sauce and popped it into my mouth. I smiled as I chewed. "This is really good, Bing," I said and paused to think. "I'm hope this cousin will have a lead for me."

CHAPTER THREE

Lian

We arrived at the apartment building which looked like it was on its last leg as a residence. I labored up the two flights of creaking, wooden stairs to the third floor. Lian's apartment left a lot to be desired; like a real lock rather than a hook and eye to hold the door shut from the outside.

"He not home," Mei said. "See door?" She pointed at the locked hook and eye.

"Any idea where he might be?" I asked.

Mei shook her head. "No," she said. "He work too many places. He busy all time."

I nodded, remembering what Bingwen had said.

"Well, now that I know where he lives, I can come back to see if he is home."

Mei's eyes widened. "No. I come with you. He no talk with you." She waggled her index finger at me. "Suspicious. He run, hide."

Again, I nodded understanding. Obviously, she knew he did some shady stuff and would run if a non-Oriental appeared at his door. Not that an Oriental person was a safe bet.

"Are you available early tomorrow morning?" I asked.

"Yes," she said. "Go to work at ten."

"Meet me here about eight. Okay?"

She nodded approval and I figured I would visit Willie when I finished. I quickly realized tomorrow morning was going to be very busy - Mei, Willie, and Zimmer. I hoped I could get it all done.

It was late so I drove Mei home which was in a much better neighborhood than Lian's place.

#

Thinking I was still young, I took the stairs, two, three at a time. Two flights later, I stood at the top of the stairs, gasping, sucking in as much air as I could. Getting my breath back, I approached Lian's apartment. Mei stood in the hallway, talking to a man who hid slightly in the open doorway. He cast a cautious look in my direction.

"This my friend," Mei said. "Barry Hargrove, this Lian, cousin."

Lian's eyes quickly scanned me up and down; no doubt his appraising me. I gave him a cursory glance and decided he was the typical Oriental, actually, almost any man who always was looking for the quick buck.

"Nice to meet you," I said before I bantered him with a barrage of questions. "What can you tell me about the Purple Dragon?"

"Purple Dragon," Lian repeated. "Big dragon. Maybe twenty, thirty men to hold it up."

I was taken aback by the number.

"Thirty?" I asked.

Lian nodded. "Three on head, then ten men, two wide, five deep next." He paused in thought. "I think another eight to ten men and then me, tail man." He paused. "Maybe more." His left eye squinted as he thought, then he nodded. "More. Yes."

I tried not to show my surprise.

"You are the tail of the Purple Dragon?"

"Yes," Lian replied.

A young woman entered the hallway from the last apartment on the opposite side. Lian nervously nodded to her as she passed. With a slight jerk of the head, he motioned us into the apartment. "Come in. Too busy to talk at door."

I allowed Mei to enter first then I followed. The door closed and a small tinkle caught my attention. Another hook and eye was on the inside to lock it. The room didn't really need a lock, there was very little worth stealing. On the floor, shoved in a corner was a mattress with a sheet trying to cover it. There was a beat-up couch daring one to sit on it. A shabby chair with well-worn fabric lingered near the window. A small table held two empty pizza boxes. A kitchen counter of maybe six feet had a sink and hot plate. Partially empty Chinese food boxes cluttered most of the counter.

The hot plate is probably the most valuable thing in the room, I thought.

The one thing that seemed out of place was the book on the edge of the couch, *Easy Sign Language*. That had me confused.

# # #

"So," I started as I leaned against the sole window sill. "How did you come to be the tail of the purple dragon?" I paused to allow him a few seconds thought, then I added. "I thought you worked the green dragon."

He nodded. "I work green dragon. Two week ago the boss tell me I no work. His son do my job." He shrugged. "You know; family first."

I nodded. *Yes, I know how that works*, I thought and gazed around the room.

"What have you been doing to pay for this place?"

"Chang Zhong, he pay me. I work purple dragon tail. Fifty dollars." He stared out the window next to me. "He say he hear I no work green dragon. I no ask questions."

I caught the innuendo; something was up.

"Why don't you ask questions? What kind of questions would you ask?"

Lian sat on the arm of the couch. It wobbled. Lian hesitated. I saw in his eyes he was working on the answer.

"Three men on head." Lian frowned. "Next ten men." He hesitated. "Maybe more. Some disappear. When purple dragon at end of parade, sometimes only four, five men remain." He shook his head. "I no see where men go. Strange." Lian held up his hands in a stop gesture. "I no ask."

"Are you aware this purple dragon has supposedly eaten young girls?" I watched as Lian formulated an answer.

He nodded. "I raise tail in sky. They say no, just swing tail back and forth." He hesitated.

"Okay, Lian," I said. "You are stalling. Spill it."

"I see body move from head to men and then the men slip

out of dragon." He shrugged. "No see them again."

"So, you saw them taking the girls," I offered.

He nodded. "Maybe girl. I no know." Lian stood and came over to where I stood and stared out the window. "Not good, but I need money."

"Are you doing the purple dragon for today's Lantern Festival parade?"

He nodded. "I go eleven to prepare." He gazed at his gold watch on his right hand.

Hm? Left-handed, I thought. To confirm my suspicion, I pulled out a sheet of paper.

"Can you write down the address?" I pushed the paper and a pen at him.

He hesitated then grabbed the pen with his left hand and wrote. He handed me the paper and pen. I gazed at the address.

How weird, I thought. *This is across the street from Chang's restaurant.*

I flicked the sheet around and showed Mei to see the address. She frowned.

"Do you recognize this address," I asked Mei.

"It across street," she replied, then shrugged.

I found her indifference a bit disconcerting. Lian worked across the street and she didn't know it. Glancing at my watch, I realized Mei needed to get to work.

"Can I come back and talk more another day?" I asked to Lian.

He nodded.

"You're not going to run?"

Lian grinned. "I no run."

I nodded to Mei and we left; I drove her to work then I had a trip to see Willie. Mei and I sat in silence in my car until it hit me.

"Mei? I noticed a book in Lian's apartment. Is he learning sign language?"

"Our cousin, Shu Fang. She come country. She deaf. He learn."

I nodded, understanding. *After all*, I thought. *Who wouldn't want to speak to their cousin?* I smiled, remembering how I learned sign language just so I could date a girl back in college. I sighed. Even though I learned to sign, she still didn't like me or date me, but we'd sign about our assignments. Since then, I've used sign language maybe six times. On a boring day, I'll go through the alphabet, signing and refresh some of the words I can remember.

CHAPTER FOUR

The Station

I ambled into the station, nodding and offering a smile to the sergeant at the desk who was 'discussing' an issue with one of the damsels of the evening. He offered me a slight nod which told me I could go on back.

Down the hall and two doors later, I walked into the 'Missing Persons' department. Third desk on the right, exactly where I expected to find him, sat my old partner, Leroy "Willie" Williamson. He was bent over the desk, intently studying something in a picture.

"What's happening?" I asked as I sat down on the chair beside the desk.

His deadpan stare at me told me everything I needed to know. He wasn't happy to see me.

"What do you want?"

I feigned shock. "What do I want?" I repeated.

"Your ugly mug only shows up when you want something."

I glanced at the pictures covering his desk. He immediately shoved them together and attempted to force them into a neat pile.

"None of your business," he mumbled, opened the top drawer of his desk and dropped them in, then closed the drawer.

"So, what you working on?" I asked.

"Again, none of your business. You're not a cop anymore." He eased back in his chair. "So, like I asked, what do you want?"

I eased around in my chair to gaze over at Preston - Detective Jim Preston. He was on the phone, eased back in his chair, feet on his desk, and pencil flipping in his fingers.

"What about Preston?" Willie whispered. "What's the issue?"

I turned back to Willie and leaned in. "Do you remember him working on a missing person, a Holly Brockwood?"

Willie squinted in thought. His eyes widened. "The dragon girl?"

I nodded. "That's the one. Her boyfriend, Zimmer, wants me to find her." Once more I sat back and glanced at Preston, then turned back to Willie. "I'm guessing Preston gave Zimmer a lot of lip service."

Willie clasped his hands together, moving them nervously. "The dragon ate her." He grinned. "Now exactly what would you do?"

I smirked. "I'd take the case... no, wait, I did take the case."

"And now you want me to give you all the information we have on the case... right?"

I smiled, placing my arm on his desk and strumming my fingers. "That would be mighty nice of you."

"Ain't going to happen," Willie said, grinning back me, his white teeth gleaming between those dark lips.

I took in a deep breath. "Not even a peek at a picture?"

Willie cocked an eye at me. "Nope. Nothing. Nada. Zip."

Shaking my head, I gave him my best pity me look. "A crumb? Remember, a dragon ate her. Don't you have anything on any rogue dragons in the area?"

His laughter filled the office and everyone was looking at us.

Preston hung up his phone. "What's so funny over there?" He got up and lumbered over. "C'mon, Willie. Share."

Willie gazed up at Preston as he approached and placed his open hands on the desk. "The dragon ate her."

Preston glared at Willie. "Not funny." He turned and stomped back to his desk.

"He thinks we're making fun of him," I said. "Probably not a good thing."

Willie shrugged. "Like I care. He's such a... a..." He drew in a deep breath. "Never mind."

I bent over and stared at my shoes and the floor. I needed some time to stop laughing.

"Tell you what," Willie whispered. "You treat for lunch and I'll get you something. Deal?"

"Meet you at Chang's, okay?" I stood and began to leave.

"The dragon ate her," Willie yelled to me.

"Shut up!" Preston screamed.

The whole office broke into laughter and I smirked as I walked out the door, knowing the bigger joke was aimed at me, not him.

CHAPTER FIVE

Chang's

Zimmer entered my office, this time as a man on a mission and immediately sat down opposite me.

With a heavy sigh, he pushed the check across the desk. "Here it is. How long do you think it will take to find Holly?"

Placing my index finger on the check, I continued to slide the check toward me, but I couldn't bring myself to tell him what I, and even Willie was thinking; young, attractive girls alone disappear in Chinatown all the time. I stalled for time.

"I'll be honest," I started. "I'd like to say I'll find her this afternoon." I shrugged. "But, reality? It could take days, even weeks to find Holly."

His eyes widened in surprise, but yet they followed the check across the desk to disappear into my top desk drawer. "Weeks?" he mumbled.

"I don't want to burst your bubble, Mr. Zimmer, but there are missing person reports that have gone on for years."

"Years?" He slumped back into the chair, the wind completely knocked out of him.

"Trust me, Mr. Zimmer." I leaned forward in an attempt to be comforting and also a confidante. "I will do everything possible to make this a short case."

He leaned forward, took my hand and shook it. "Thank you, Detective Hargrove. I will wait for your report. You have my number."

James Zimmer stood, appearing more mature than when he walked in, turned, and left the office.

I opened the top drawer and looked at the check. *Yes! I am definitely able to treat Willie to lunch. Thank you, Mr. Zimmer.*

# # #

Willie slid into the booth, sitting opposite me. "Wow! Nice digs. When did Bingwen change all this around?"

I nodded. "I'm thinking the first of the week. He has definitely put his mark on his old man's restaurant. By the way, I ordered you sweet and sour chicken with extra sauce, chicken fried rice, and an egg roll. Hope you don't mind. I also got you your Ginger Tea."

He slipped a manila folder toward me and nodded. "You're a good man, Barry." He began to grin. "And, I'll deny those words if you ever claim I said it. Now, do you have no idea how long it took to get everyone back into office mode." He bent his head down and shook it. "Preston was so ticked. I wouldn't suggest you visit for quite some time; he thinks you're the culprit."

"Not a whole lot he can do to me," I said while taking the folder. "Remember, I'm no longer a cop, just a civilian."

Willie snorted and put his large black hand on the folder, stopping me. "No, but he can put your pathetic butt in the slammer for a short length of time for no other reason than he just feels you need it."

I shrugged. He had me on that point. I tugged on the folder and he removed his hand.

"What is this?" I asked, opening the folder.

Mei approached. "Two sweet sour chicken." She placed the plates on the table.

"Thank you," Willie said.

"Xièxiè, (thank you)" I said.

Mei smiled, bowed and stepped away. "Enjoy."

Willie dug into the sweet and sour. "As always, excellent food."

"Who you trying to suck up to?" Looking up, I saw Bingwen standing at the table. "Yes, as always, excellent."

"You didn't order khorkhog and Jasmine tea?" He gazed at me. "What's up? Not feeling well?"

I nodded to my companion. "He like sweet and sour chicken,

and, of course, Ginger Tea."

Bingwen nodded. "Ah, yes, Detective Williamson. I remember now, he doesn't like khorkhog, an acquired taste."

I leaned back on my chair. "Like a fine, aged scotch. You need to acquire the taste."

"And that's a bunch of bull," Willie said between bites. He thumped his index finger on the table. "You bring me a shot of Chevis Regal and any other brand; I'll tell you which is which." He grinned. "I know a good scotch when I taste it."

Bingwen turned and spoke Chinese to the bartender. He had a sly grin on his face and he was turned so Willie couldn't see him, Bingwen winked at me. The bartender approached the table with two shots of scotch whiskey and placed them before Willie.

"Okay, Detective Williamson, you tell me which of these is the Chevis," Bingwen said.

Willie stopped eating and lifted one shot glass to his nose and lightly inhaled the fragrance. He glanced at the color of the liquid in the glass, then he tasted.

"I'm pretty sure this is Chevis," he said and lifted the second shot glass and sniffed. Once more he glanced at the color of the whiskey and then tasted.

"Nope. This is the Chevis Regal." He held the empty shot glass in the air. "I can tell by the taste. Smooth. Smokey. Earthy." He squinted in thought. "An oakiness, as well."

I stared at Willie. *When did he become a connoisseur of scotch whiskey?*

Bingwen shrugged. "To be quite honest, that is an Ardbeg twenty-five-year-old scotch from Scotland. I hope you enjoyed it; the cost is a mere sixty dollars a shot."

My head jerked around and I stared at Bingwen. *Did he expect me to pay for that taste test?*

Willie held up the empty Chevis Regal shot glass to his nose. "I originally told you this was Chevis, but I got bamboozled by an over-priced scotch." Willie's eyes sparkled in devilment. "For the cost..." He held up the empty Chevis shot glass. "This is my preference." With a slight shrug and a sly grin, he added. "Call me cheap."

"Shut up and eat your stupid sweet and sour," I said.

"Don't worry, Detective Hargrove," Bingwen said. "I won't charge you for the scotch. I ordered the shots." He turned and walked away to meet new customers just entering the restaurant.

"Thank you, Bingwen," I whispered to the distancing figure and shoved another bite of fried rice into my mouth. My eyes kept straying to the manila folder.

Willie put his fork down and leaned over the table. "Do you want me to tell you what's in that folder?"

"If you want." I cocked my head to the side. "I'm going to look at it sooner or later."

He sighed. "Simple. There are eight missing young ladies in the folder. Most of them disappearing during Chinese parades."

Willie stared at me, waiting.

"Let me guess," I said. "All eaten by a dragon."

"No." The voice was deadpan. "But all were assigned to Preston who couldn't see or find a way to connect them together."

"But," I started. "You did?"

"No." Again, Willie's voice was deadpan. "They are all missing. Some were taken during the Chinese holidays; others seem to just come up missing." He shrugged. "Preston gave it what I call 'the old college try' which means after thirty seconds, give up."

I nodded. "My client got that feeling. Zimmer didn't care for Preston." I hesitated. "By the way, who is bantering my name around the office; that's how Zimmer got my name."

"Preston. He's a jerk," Willie said. "Figures your private detective skills would break this case wide open." He leaned in over his plate. "Wouldn't it be neat if you could."

I shrugged. "That's why I make the big bucks." I scooped another forkful of fried rice into my mouth.

"Now." Willie grabbed the folder. "Here's the pictures and what information we have on each of the missing girls." He picked up his egg roll and began to munch. "This is Holly Brockwood." He gazed at the picture. "She sure is a pretty girl."

"And a virgin," I added.

He cocked an eye at me. "A virgin? Are you thinking what I'm thinking?"

I nodded. "Trafficking."

"Crap! Why do I think you're right?" Willie spread the other pictures between us on the table. "I wonder how many of these others are or were virgins?"

"You haven't said your favorite phrase, yet." I grinned at him.

"You mean, share your information?"

I nodded. "Seems Holly here..." I lifted the picture. "She was ate by a purple dragon. I was able to make a connection with one of the handlers." I paused. "You ready?"

"What?" Willie stared at me, frozen in time, holding the last piece of his egg roll.

"The purple dragon people gather right across the street in that warehouse-like building." I paused, knowing Willie was hanging on my every word. "In fact, they're meeting there..." I looked at my watch. "Right about now."

My old partner got that look I knew all too well. "Do we bust in after lunch?" He grinned. "You know, check things out."

"You game?" I asked.

He gazed at his plate. "A couple more bites, I'm done and we are so out of here."

I laughed. "You're too eager, Willie."

"Hey, if we could break this case, just think how Preston will look." He took a deep breath. "Anything to put that jerk in his place."

I lifted my cup of Ginger tea. "To partners."

Willie lifted his cup and we toasted, then drank.

CHAPTER SIX

The Warehouse

Exciting out of Chang's, shoving the double red dragon doors open, I stared at the building across the street when Willie stated the obvious.

"Don't look much like a warehouse. Of course, it doesn't look like much of an office building, either."

The old brick structure stood silent, showing the years of non-use. The building obviously was built during the 1920s or 1930s because of the art deco detailing. I stared at the structure. *Had it had a facelift? Was the art deco added?* I thought.

"Well," I said, taking off across the street. "We can look at the stupid building or we can go in. Coming?"

"This should prove interesting," Willie mumbled and followed me.

Now, standing in front of the tall structure, I realized, I had never, in all my years of eating at Chang's, ever taken notice of this building. *Not a very good detective, Barry*, I thought, chastising myself.

I strode up to the door and pulled the handle.

It opened. I frowned. *Is it still in use?*

Willie, again, stated the obvious. "Didn't expect that."

A sky-bound firework exploded, startling me.

I pulled the door open, we walked in, and now stood in the middle of a run-down art deco lobby. There was a heavy wooden desk in the center of the room, but there was nobody in attendance. Dust covered the desk, along with a Tiffany-style lamp, and what appeared to be a ledger book.

Reaching down with my fingertip, I caught the edge and lifted the corner of the book. The pages were yellow.

It was my turn; I stated the obvious. "Hasn't been used in a very long time."

Willie nodded.

I let the cover of the book drop back down. A small cloud of dust billowed around it. I shrugged.

"Do you hear that?" Willie asked.

Faint sounds. People talking.

I motioned with a jerk of my head for Willie to follow and we stealthily moved toward the sound.

The muffled voices clarified. I could understand them. It was Chinese. Willie gave me a blank stare. I know some Chinese, but not what one would call fluent. I listened and grasped what I could understand, trying to put it into some context.

"It is like they're training," I whispered. "They are trying to organize who does what."

Willie nodded.

I noticed a wall with windows. The windows hadn't been cleaned in ages and were covered in grime, dirt, and dust. It was almost impossible to see through, but there were a few broken areas where one could see into the room where the men worked. I motioned for Willie to follow me and we silently made our way there.

I was happy. I could not only hear, but also see what was going on.

Three men manipulated the huge head of the purple dragon.

"I tongue." The more muscular of the three men spoke. "I lick girl. I decide I pull girl in." He turned to a group of men. "Shing. Li. You take girl, hold her, then take her out to street. Bao. Chang. You take next girl. We only do two girls tonight." The men nodded their heads.

The tongue man turned to the man under the tail and raised his voice. "You! Tail man. You new. You move tail back and forth, not up and down. We water dragon, not sky dragon."

The dragon tail swung to the side and Lian, Mei's cousin stepped out from under it, holding the pole for the tail. "Yes. Understood." He bowed.

I motioned for Willie to follow and we headed back out of the building. On the street, I relayed the information of what the leader had said. I considered sharing the small detail of Mei's cousin being the tail man, but decided against it.

"I can have a team out tonight to watch and snag them," he said.

"That would be good, but we haven't found my missing person." I stood there rubbing my chin in thought. "I hate the possibility of losing another girl, but let me follow them and see if I can find where they are hiding them. Plus, do you really want to arrest the whole dragon team? I don't think all of them know what is happening." I didn't want to share, but... "That tail man is... Mei, remember our waitress? That's her cousin and he's been my informant. He knew the girls were being dragged in, but thought they were being released."

Willie stood there, weaving, definitely hm-hawing what to do.

"I shouldn't allow this, but I trust you, Barry, and will give you a little slack. But, if you mess this up, you're going down, too." He shook his head. "Why do I keep doing this? I'm going to get my black ass fired.

In the distance a round of firecrackers filled the air.

CHAPTER SEVEN

The Files

I returned to the office and sat at my desk, the files Willie had given me were spread out to review. I frowned. Some of the girls had been missing almost three years. *Why did Willie include them?* I had to find the connection. Picking up the oldest picture, Jessie Elridge, 23, missing three years and 2 months. Attended the Chinese New Year parade. Disappeared.

I grabbed the next picture. Amanda Stellows, 20, missing two years and 8 months, June fifth.

My mind played with the date. *Why that date? Ah! The fifth day of the fifth lunar month; the Chinese Boat Festival.*

It hit me. Three years! The guys in the purple dragon had been absconding with young girls for over three years! It didn't make sense. The purple dragon was a new dragon; maybe only a year old, at best from what I'd been able to find out.

I nodded, understanding now why Jim Preston was having issues trying to tie all these missing reports together. The only tie-in was the fact they are happened in Chinatown and usually during a festival.

Picking up the third picture, I noticed the girl had a Chinese tattoo for good luck above her wrist. Sort of ironic. Susan North, 21, missing for two years and two months. I scratched my head. There was no festival or holiday around that time. It was before the Chinese New Year. A fluke?

I worked my way through the remaining pictures; some girls missing during a festival; some not. I shook my head. No rhyme, no reason. I grinned. *Poor Jim, definitely a frustration level.* Now the question was simple; could I figure it out and find the girls, if they still were in the area.

Leaning back in my chair, I pressed my thumb and index finger against the bridge of my nose and gave it a small massage.

"These girls are the victims of a white-slave trade," I whispered in a mumble. *I might find Holly, but the others, it is probably too late*, I thought. My mind flashed. *White-slave trade... or, is it sex-slave trade? If the latter, Holly had a chance of lingering in the area until they got all the buyers together. She was a virgin, or so Mr. Zimmer claimed, and something told me, it was a truth.*

I put the files in a chronological order with Holly Brockwood on top and Jessie Elridge on the bottom. I put the file in my desk drawer and glanced at the clock: 4:46 p.m.

Best get myself going, I thought and headed out of the office, carefully locking the door behind me. Had Chinese for lunch... I shrugged. Could enjoy some khorkhog, but instead, I decided to see if Juan's Taco, the street vendor was still available. Stepping into the late afternoon sunlight, at the corner, like a fixture locked in time, was Juan and his portable taco stand. My mouth started to drool at the thought of the greasy tacos and nacho chips slathered with all that fake cheese. I waved as I strolled down the steps and headed toward Juan.

"Ah, señor Hargrove," Juan said. "You want three beef taco, one nacho chips with extra cheese, and a root beer. Si?"

"You know me, Juan." I nodded approval. "You taking the family to the parade tonight?"

"Oh, no, señor," Juan sputtered. "Marissa, my wife, she say we attend school function. Jorge in play."

"A play? Jorge?" My mind stretched to remember Jorge's age; maybe seven or eight. "What is the name of the play?"

Juan cast an indifferent glance. "I think it called Three Little Pigs. Jorge play the bad wolf."

"Quite an honor there, Juan. Jorge is the star."

"Si." Juan responded. "What you do tonight?"

"A little reconnaissance," I said. "Working a missing person. She..."

"Ah, no buena, (not good) señor Hargrove." He glanced in each direction. "Girls not safe in Chinatown. I no bring my daughters here." Juan nodded. "New Year Festival, young man come here, he buy two pops and chips. Soon he back asking if girlfriend came. He yelling she ate by dragon." Juan shook his head. "Poor boy." He put his index finger up to the side of his head and made a repeating circle. "He crazy, I think." He snickered. "Dragon ate her." He pointed up into the sky. "No dragons here."

I silently nodded, not seeing any reason to tell Juan that was my case now. I forced a laugh, paid Juan, and took my food. "Buenos noches," (good night) I said.

"Buenos noches, señor Hargrove."

I headed up the street toward Chinatown. I gave a quick glance back at Juan who was shutting his umbrella and closing up business for the night. I shoved another taco bite into my mouth. *Lord, these are so good*, I thought.

I wandered the streets of Chinatown. It would be at least another hour before the parade started. I stood in front of a Chinese candy store, Jin's Treats, watching Shen Jin make Dragon Beard candy. I watched as he stretched the hoop of strands, folded, stretched, folded; each time making the strands finer and finer. Chen Li smiled and nodded at me then jerked his head for me to come into the store.

"Nǐhǎo," (hello) I said as I entered.

"Almost done, only fifteen more stretch," Shen Jin said. "See son, already made Dragon Beard earlier." He grinned, his crooked teeth gleaming. "Special today. Twelve pieces, price of ten."

"At a price like that, how can I refuse?" I ambled back to the counter where Liang Jin stood by the cash register.

"Nǐhǎo," (hello) Liang Jin said. "You buy Dragon Beard?"

"Two orders," I said. "They melt in your mouth and don't last too long, except for the peanut center." I opened my wallet to get the money out. "These taste so much better than that flavored cotton candy the street vendor sells."

Liang Jin made a face. "He no make good candy." He nodded to the older man in the window stretching the strands of spun sugar.

"Baba (father) make best candy. Authentic Dragon Beard."

I paid and grabbed the bag of small nuggets of deliciousness. *Will these last until the parade?* I thought.

"*Xièxiè,*" (thank you) I said and exited the building, waving to Shen Jin as he continued to stretch the sugar strands.

Fireworks continued to light up the sky and firecrackers exploded here and there. The Chinese Lantern Festival was about to start.

CHAPTER EIGHT

The Parade

I stood with the mobs lining the street as the parade began. I situated myself near an attractive young Caucasian girl. It was the only thing all the girls who were missing had in common, other than missing. All indications showed she was alone; I saw no boyfriend or husband.

I waited.

The purple dragon danced toward us, the huge head bobbing up, down, and side to side. Every so often the tongue lashed out. I watched it lick a couple of people — a young man, an old woman, a child. Then it was in front of me and as I suspected, it licked the young girl. She laughed.

In a quick motion, the head lifted and then engulfed her; she disappeared.

The dragon ate her!

The parade patrons laughed and applauded, but none were concerned.

I followed, waiting for the supposed release.

The side of the dragon lifted and three bodies moved away from the dragon. They were all dressed alike, wearing purple robes to match the dragon.

I frowned. The middle person seemed groggy, exhausted. The two on either side carried the... it was the girl!

Being discreet, I stayed back and followed as the trio wove a path through the mass of bodies straining to watch the parade.

Suddenly, fireworks lit the sky in an array of colors: red, green, blue, pink, gold, and silver.

The parade had hit its zenith. The next ten minutes were nothing but bolts of colored lights in the sky, ricocheting blasts, and annoying firecrackers everywhere. The people clustered together, oohing and aahing, making it difficult to move. But, I persevered, as did the three I was following.

Finally, we were clear of the mob and I kept the trio just within my eyesight, following them as they struggled to keep the girl upright between them. They turned a corner into an alley. I raced to peek around the corner.

They were gone.

Nothing. An empty alley.

Oh, Willie is going to slammer me and enjoy the moment, I thought.

I ambled down the alley with its limited light. Everything was either dark or in shadows.

To my immediate right was a door with a padlocked hinge.

Hm, didn't go that way, I thought.

I scanned the alley. Dead end. Two more doors. I walked up to the first. Again, a padlock. I ambled to the other door. There was no padlock so I tried to open the door, turning the knob, I pushed. It didn't budge. I pulled and the door opened toward me.

Stepping back, I allowed the door to open completely. What I didn't expect, greeted me. The entry was completely sealed with a brick wall. Hoping for the best, I pushed. It didn't give. That wall had been there for some time.

Once more I glanced about the alley. The only other object was the big metal dumpster.

Ah-ha! I thought.

With a heavy grunt, and a major strain of my body's muscles, I pushed the dumpster away from the wall.

I was met with a full wall and no opening. I leaned against the dumpster, sweating, attempting to get my wind back.

Where in the hell did they go? My mind screamed, wanting an answer. Again, I surveyed the area. Nothing seemed out of place.

Yes, Willie is going to hang me up by... I realized then I needed another to look at this conundrum.

I reached for my phone. *Damn! Left it in the office.* I shook my head in disgust.

I hustled back to the street and gazed up and down, ascertaining my whereabouts. The Handy Dandy Family Pharmacy was two blocks away and I knew Chen would let me use his phone.

It was a quick run to Chen's place and he greeted me almost immediately upon my entrance.

"Can I use your phone?" I asked.

He nodded and pointed to the phone on the counter by the checkout.

I called Willie.

"Hello?" A young girl's voice answered.

"Hi..." My mind raced to remember which daughter I was talking to. *Bella is the older at six,* I thought. *Stella is the younger, only four.* "Bella. Is your daddy home?"

"Daddy!" I heard her yell. "Telephone."

"Hello?" It was Willie.

"I need your help. Meet me at Chen's Handy Dandy Family Pharmacy. They took a girl and I lost her."

"What did I tell you?" Willie said.

"I know where I lost her. It was a dead end alley. Now get over here." I hung up, not waiting for an answer.

# # #

Ten minutes later, I was finishing a coffee, talking with Chen at the door when Willie drove up to the curb. I handed Chen my cup and left the store.

"One block straight ahead, take a left, one more block and in the next block, the alley to your right."

"So, you lost the victim," Willie said.

"No, I didn't lose her. I know exactly where she is." I grinned. "I just don't where they went."

Willie pulled into the alley, the car's headlights shining on the dead end, lighting everything.

"It's obvious," Willie said, noting the alley and doorways. "They went in one of the doors."

I grinned. "Great observation. I would never have thought of that."

Willie gave me a dead-pan glare. "Let's check it out."

He turned off the car, the lights going out and everything was in darkness.

"Get me the flashlight out of the glove box," Willie said.

I handed him the flashlight and we got out of the car.

He headed for the first door with the padlocked hinge. Willie waved the light around the door's perimeter and we stared at the padlock.

"Didn't go this way," he said and headed for the next door.

He held the light on the padlock.

"Hm?" He reached out and tested the lock. It was secure. "Last door?"

I tried not to laugh. "You're going to enjoy the next door. It's open."

Again, Willie gave me a glare. I shrugged.

Like me, he turned the knob and pushed, then pulled. The door opened and Willie snapped the flashlight up. The brick wall behind the door reflected the light.

"Huh," Willie grunted and pushed against the bricks. Like before, they didn't move.

I leaned against the wall with my arms folded over my chest, rather proud of myself.

"This is why I called you. They came in this alley, I followed. They were gone, but where?" I stretched out my arms to encompass the area. "I know they didn't fly up."

To be sure of my statement, I glanced up to make sure I hadn't missed anything. There were no fire escapes or ladders to be seen. I gazed at Willie.

"You know," I started. "We tried both these doors...." I nodded at the first door, the one with the padlocked hinge. "Maybe we should try it."

Willie shrugged. "Why not." He strolled to the door and picked up the padlock and pulled. The lock didn't give. He frowned as he realized the hinge moved away from the door jam. He pulled the hinge away and we heard a click.

"Did the door unlock?" I asked.

Willie turned the door knob and the door opened.

"I think I know where they disappeared," I said and stepped into the darkness of the door way.

CHAPTER NINE

Discovery

Willie turned the flashlight into the open area.

"Turn that off," I whispered. "No reason to let them see us coming."

Willie turned off the flashlight and we worked our way through the dimly lit area.

In the distance I could hear voices; they were indistinct. I thought I could discern a couple of men's voices, and, I wasn't sure, but there seemed to be a number of women's voices.

I approached a corner; the voices were stronger and a light shone into the hallway in front of me.

"How many Zhong take tonight?" It was a man's voice in the room down the short hallway.

"Bao and Chang should be here soon," another voice said.

I recognized the names and remember they were to get the second victim. Behind us I heard a struggling girl and two men grunting in their attempts to control her.

I grabbed Willie's arm and pulled him into the room across from us, hoping no one would come in there. I placed a finger to my lips to indicate to Willie to be quiet. He nodded.

We listened and the new trio struggled past where we hid.

"Bao! Chang!" the first voice called.

I motioned to Willie and we once more stepped out into the hallway.

A heated discussion ensued in Chinese, pushing my limits on what I understood. Willie kept nudging me, wanting to know what they were saying. I peeked around the corner; there were five men in the room. I saw two women off in a corner, in a cell-like containment area. I frowned.

Words came to me that I recognized, but four caught my attention: door, lock, car, alley.

I realized what they were having a heated discussion about. When Willie and I came into the building, I don't remember either of us closing the door behind us. Willie's car was sitting in the alley. I was pretty sure they thought somebody else was in the building other than them.

Pushing Willie, I led the way back out of the building. The door was closed. I grabbed Willie's flashlight and discovered the spring mechanism to keep the door shut. I opened the door, pushed Willie out, and quickly closed it behind me as I exited.

"Why you pushing me around?" Willie asked.

"Simple," I replied. "We forgot to shut the door behind us when we entered. They realized somebody else was in the building. Plus, your car was in the alley which also caused suspicion."

Willie nodded. "Get in the car and let's get out of here. We need some backup."

I got in the car. "First things first. No backup. Let me scope the situation. There were five men in there, plus I saw the two women they abducted."

Willie glared at me in the darkness. "We know where they are and can save those women."

I shrugged. "Not really. We know they are here right now, but they could take them elsewhere. Tell you what, you go home. I'll stay here and keep an eye on what happens. If they take the girls someplace else, I'll let you know."

"Everything is telling me to ignore your request, follow my gut, and get backup." Willie backed the car out of the alley. "Where to?" he asked.

"Actually, right here. Stop the car and let me out. I'll do surveillance."

Willie stopped the car and stared at me. "Right. You're going to be the innocent man on the corner of the building, smoking a cigarette, looking nonchalantly around the area." Willie pushed his arm past me and toward my window. "Look out there, Barry. There ain't nothing but nothing. You'd stick out like a moon pie at a pretzel convention." He started to put the car back into gear.

I opened the door and stepped out before he applied the gas. "I will attempt to be more subtle than that."

"Your funeral," Willie said. "See you in the morning. I'll stop by with coffee."

"And donuts," I added.

Willie drove off and I headed back into the alley. Ambling over to the dumpster, I dug around in it until I found exactly what I wanted — an old newspaper and some cardboard. I smeared some dark grease on my face. I considered camping out across from the door but decided that was too obvious. I put the cardboard in the corner where the dumpster and building met. Hunkering down, curling against the building, I arranged the newspapers over me to create my blanket. I waited.

CHAPTER TEN

Zhong's Plans

It was forty minutes of pretending to be asleep when the long, black sedan pulled into the alley, the headlights nearly blinding me. I curled deeper into my huddle, hoping they would ignore me. I kept my eyes to a near slit, barely able to see anything.

Chang Zhong stepped from the car and pointed at me. "Who he?" He lifted his arm and with his thumb, motioned for me to be removed out of the ally. "Gone."

Two thugs came toward me.

"Homeless," one of them said. "He harmless. He sleep."

The other came over and kicked me. "You go. Gone."

I faked waking up and cowering. I nodded.

Zhong nodded and the thugs turned and followed him to the door. Zhong fiddled with the lock, making sure if anyone was watching, like me, that he was unlocking the door. He pushed it open and the three men entered. The door shut.

I sprang into action, tossing my blanket of newspapers to the side, I stood up. My mind immediately realized, there could still be others in the car.

I waited. Nothing.

I approached the door and pulled the hinge and listened to the spring snap. The door opened and I entered the dark world of the hallway, remembering to close the door behind me. This time I knew where I was going, it was faster and easier. The voices in the distance helped guide me.

"You wait two hours," Zhong said. "Take to Jin's place. He waiting."

I approached the corner where I could hear and see into the room.

Jin's place? I thought. *Did he mean Shen Jin's candy store? No, wait. There's more than one Jin in the community. It had to be somebody else. Shen was a nice, old guy.*

"Five girls," Zhong continued. "We sell." The leer on Zhong's face chilled me. "One virgin." He rubbed his hands together, his eyes sparkling. "Much money for her."

He started toward me, stopped and turned to the men in the room.

"Clean room. Purple dragon next three parades, no girls. We sell girls, clean room. No trace."

And that is why Preston had so much trouble... no continuity, I thought. *They're going to lay low.*

Once more Zhong headed my way. I slipped into the dark office across from my hiding place where Willie and I hid earlier. My only hope was Zhong wouldn't come in.

I squatted in the far corner, watching the shadowy silhouettes of Zhong and his two henchmen on the office windows. They passed and I waited, listening to the remaining four men in the other room. I shuffled to the door and opened it a crack.

"No!" a woman screamed.

I watched one man push the needle into her arm as another man held her. She fought for a second, then slumped in her chair where she was tied.

The other girl watched; her eyes wide with fear. She frantically searched for an escape, but like the other, she was tied to the chair.

"Not much," the man on the left of the guy with the needle said. "She need walk."

The man with the needle nodded and pushed the hypodermic needle into the girl's arm. A few seconds later her head swung around, she was trying to focus, to hold her head up. The drug, whatever it was, gave the impression she was drunk.

A third guy shoved the hood over her head. It was then I noticed the other girl had a hood on her head already, the fourth guy watching her.

"Bao," the third guy called. "You, me, we take her."

I tried to remember the names. If I remembered correctly, it was Shing and Li who took the first girl, the girl now groggy in the chair. Bao and Chang had the second girl who was knocked out.

"Go!" Bao said and stretched the girl's one arm over his neck and shoulder. The other, I assumed to be Chang, did the same with the other arm and the girl was now between the two men.

They headed toward me and I scurried to the office to let them pass. Shing and Li had the other girl between them and she attempted to walk with them. I waited and then followed. They shut the outside door and I waited, allowing them time to get away from the door. I opened it and saw them turn to the left out of the alley. They were headed back toward the parade route.

I shook my head. *This is not good*, I thought. *They're headed to Jin's place.* I lifted my eyes to the sky. *Please go another way.*

Strolling nonchalantly behind the group, I kept a safe distance so they wouldn't realize I was following. They ignored me and turned on the street of Jin's Treats. I shook my head.

Before entering the block with Jin's Treats, they turned, again. I sighed relief.

It was momentary. They turned into the alley and went directly to the back door of Jin's Treats. *Was that Liang who opened the door as they approached?* My mind raced. With the shadows, I couldn't be sure. Whoever it was, he kept scanning the area as the six entered the store. I remained in the shadows of the alley across the street.

Was Shen involved? Such a nice, old guy. I shook my head in disgust. *Obviously, Liang was involved.*

I walked across the street and entered the alley, quickly accessing the door to Jin's Treats. Turning the knob, I couldn't believe my luck. The door was unlocked. That indicated two things; either Jin didn't expect anyone to break in, or... I held my breath; they were expecting another person.

Sweat broke out as I realized I could get caught between those in the store already and anyone who might come later. My mind raced to think of who and Zhong came to mind. I shivered, grabbed the knob and opened the door, throwing caution to the wind.

You're in this deep, I thought. *What else could possibly happen? What could go wrong?*

I focused on what I needed to do, not what could happen.

Voices came from below me. I realized they were in the basement. Some of the stores had basements; Shen was lucky to have the extra storage. I stood at the top of the stairs, debating on whether to go down or stay where I was.

The back door slammed shut. Somebody had entered.

CHAPTER ELEVEN

The Basement

I heard Zhong's voice as he told his thugs to stay by the back door. Slipping behind the open basement door, I held it tight against me, letting me hide behind in the small triangle of space.

Zhong stomped down the steps.

I came back around and watched his shadowed figure finish the steps and walk to the left where the light was the strongest.

Analyzing the situation, I realized I was between the proverbial rock and hard place. My only safety net was the cubby behind the door, but that didn't allow me to see what was happening and who all was in the basement. As Caesar said at the Rubicon River, the die is cast.

I started down the stairs, taking each one softly and slowly, praying none would give away my presence. I was about to take another step when I realized my foot would be visible. I held back, grabbing the handrail, I leaned down to peek and see what I could.

I counted.

Six men, four in dragon robes, Zhong, and Liang. Five women in small steel cages. I immediately recognized the two from tonight, the third was none other than Holly Brockwood. The other two I recognized from the files.

"Secretary tell buyers," Zhong said. "They be here tomorrow night. Auction proceed." He turned to the girls in the cages and leered. "One is virgin. Others? Prove it?" He shrugged and rolled his hands over each other. "You bring more money and... uh... good owner?"

"You want a virgin? I'm a virgin," one of the new girls said.

"Me, too," said the other new girl.

"And me," said another from behind in a cage.

The new girl glared at the other two. "Bring a real doctor and I can prove it."

"For money..." Zhong leered. "A doctor here morning." He paused. "You not, you first sell. First offer buy you. Sold."

"I am a virgin," the girl repeated. Softly, under her breath, she added, "Anything to allow me some time to figure out how to get free."

"Okay," Zhong said. "Two virgins. Very lucky."

"What are you going to do with us?" Holly asked.

"Obvious," Zhong replied. "I sell you highest bidder. Customers international; some in flight here." He grinned and rubbed his hands together. "They take you home. They decide their business. I offer merchandise."

Holly stepped back in her cage.

"So, we're being sold as sex slaves," one of other girls I couldn't remember the name of, but recognized from the files. "What makes you think we won't run away?"

Zhong cast a glance at the wall. "See them? Slow you down."

I glanced in the direction he looked. On the wall, heavy black metal shackles and ball and chains hung, waiting.

"You wouldn't dare," the girl said.

Zhong put a finger to his lips. "Dare? You in cage. I dare."

The girl grabbed the bars of her cage and tried to shake them. The cage barely moved.

"No exhaust you," Zhong sneered. "You look good tomorrow night." Zhong leaned toward the cage. "Yes, Giovanni Pirozzi, he pay plenty." Laughing, he headed for the stairs. "Bao. Li. You stay tonight. You other two come in morning relieve." He turned to Liang. "I be back ten thirty tomorrow." He gazed at the girls. "We make sure look good for auction." He sighed. "Ten-dollar makeup bring extra grand or two."

Giovanni Pirozzi, I thought. *That name I recognize*. A plan formed.

I heard Holly whimpering, but also heard Zhong's steps move toward the staircase. I silently rushed up the stairs and around the door to hide.

"You sure father no idea?" Zhong asked.

"Baba (father) no knowledge. I go to basement."

It was Liang's voice. I was relieved. *Shen has no idea what is happening in the bowels of his store*, I thought. *He just sits in the window and makes Dragon's Beard*. I watched through the crack as the two men approached the top of the steps.

"Stay that way next twenty-four hours," Zhong said, thumping his forefinger on Liang's chest.

Liang pushed away Zhong's hand. "No issue."

"Ha! Correct phrase no problem, but..." Zhong grimaced. and headed for the back door. "Come," he ordered his thugs.

I waited, holding my breath. *Will Liang come and close the basement door?* My mind raced as Liang approached the basement steps then turned and headed into the store.

Without realizing it, I'd held my breath. I exhaled. The sound of another set of footsteps on the basement stairs caught my attention.

"Li, I find food." He laughed. "Plenty candy."

"No candy, Bao." The words echoed up the basement staircase hallway.

I held my breath as Bao strolled by my hiding place behind the door.

Exactly how do you get out of this, Barry? I thought.

There wasn't a whole lot of time to figure out my situation. Bao came shuffling back, grabbed the door knob, pulling the door to the basement behind him as he headed down the stairs.

I stood open to the world, stuffed in the corner. I needed to act and act fast. Glancing at the back door, I realized there was only one choice.

I took it.

CHAPTER TWELVE

Plotting A Plan

I called Willie. I knew it was late and he would be ticked, but still, something needed to be done. I could have called Preston and let him get the glory, but why? He was a jerk and I never liked him when I was on the police force.

Willie answered the phone. "Hello?" he mumbled, half asleep.

"This is Barry and..."

"This better be good," Willie snarled.

"You need a cup of coffee," I said. "Meet me at Handy Dandy. I'll have one ready for you." I hung up.

I hope he shows, I thought. *If he doesn't, I'll still make a plan.*

The Handy Dandy 24-hour sign glowed in the distance. *Always open*, I thought. *Chen wants to make every penny he can.*

I wondered who ran the store at night since his daughter killed herself that night by impaling herself on the sword Chen had kept above the door. I shrugged.

Stepping into the store, I was greeted by Chen. I frowned.

"Ah, Detective Hargrove," Chen said with a sincere smile. "You need picture develop?"

"No," I said and shook my head. "Just in for coffee and waiting for Willie to show." I ambled over to the counter, sliding onto the stool as he poured me a cup of coffee.

"Put another out," I said and pointed to an empty place beside me. "Willie is coming."

The front door opened and I turned to see Willie glaring at me as he approached. Above him I saw the Jian sword above the door. I hadn't noticed before, but it was now heavily secured to the wall. It still held a place of honor.

Chen's not taking any chances, I thought.

Willie straddled the stool at the counter beside me, pulling the coffee closer, diluting it with too much cream and loading it with sugar packets.

"Have you considered non-sugar replacements?" I asked.

"None of your business, Barry." He glared at me. "Now, what is so damned important I'm here drinking coffee when I should be in bed beside my wife and getting my beauty sleep."

I gently patted the side of his face. "You look good enough, no need for the sleep."

Willie rolled his eyes. "Give."

"The auction is going down tomorrow..." I glanced at the clock. "Uh, tonight at that warehouse."

Willie sipped his coffee, set the cup down, and looked directly at me. He took a deep breath.

"Your plan?"

I smiled. "Do you recognize the name Giovanni Pirozzi?"

Willie frowned. "He's some Italian perfume designer."

"That's him and you know me. Always a plan, but ever ready to adjust if necessary. Zhong has five girls ready to auction tonight. As we speak, the buyers are being notified." I frowned. "Not sure how many buyers... could be two, could be twenty." I shrugged. "He has two virgins Zhong figures will bring in big bucks, so the buyers I figure aren't local, that much, I'm sure."

"And what do we do?" Again, Willie lifted the cup of coffee and slurped.

Of his many bad habits, that was one that always irritated me the most. He could sip his coffee and that was fine, but when he slurped, it was like the sound of a tsunami hitting the LA skyline. It grated on me... and he knew that. I ignored it.

"I figure you can have a couple of people posted in the back. Have a couple of squad cars about two blocks out." I envisioned my plan. "I will be in the alley as a street person so I can see who all comes in." I paused. "When we are sure the auction has started, you have the squad cars move in — quietly, no sirens or lights — and we surround the warehouse."

Willie turned on his booth so his back was to the counter; he leaned back.

"If I get this to fly," he started. "And you're wrong..." He stared off to the distance. "My ass goes on the block, I get busted down to janitor, my retirement is lost, and you continue to play detective."

"And, if I am right," I countered. "This could be quite a feather to put in your cap." I paused; I was about to play my big card. "Plus, you get to show up Preston who couldn't bust this case."

Willie burst into a full-blown laugh. "You had me at feather, but your Preston card pushed me over the edge. I'm in." He flipped around and gulped the last of the light-brown syrupy coffee down. "I'll get things started." He paused. "I wonder who the judge is for tonight?" He shrugged. "Doesn't matter. I'll get the paperwork going."

I slapped Willie on the back. "Like old times?" I asked.

"Don't even go there, Barry," he said. "How many times did you hang me out to dry? This better go down or I will be on you even your shadow will be ashamed to follow."

"More coffee?" Chen asked.

"No thanks, Chen," Willie said and covered his cup with his hand. "I got work to do." He slid off the stool and headed out.

Chen motioned to pour coffee for me. Shaking my head, I followed Willie.

Giovanni Pirozzi stewed in his chair; his hands strumming the table. I walked into the room with Willie.

Pirozzi lifted a hand into the air, the index finger waving back and forth. "You no can hold me," Giovanni said. "I am citizen of Italy."

Willie stayed in the shadows near the door.

I nodded at Giovanni. "We suspect, with viable reports, that you have come into our country on false pretenses."

Giovanni pulled himself upright, puffing himself to get as large as possible to intimidate me.

"I come to city. I want open restorant. I visit Buona Luna

Italiana." He grinned. "Best Italian in town."

"So, you want to steal the chef from Buona Luna Italiana; is that what you're saying."

"I no steal," Giovanni snapped, losing some of his puffiness, turning to stare off in the distance.

"I take it you didn't plan to visit Chinatown?"

Giovanni jerked his head to glare at me.

His forehead wrinkled in a frown. "Why I go to Chinatown?" He smiled. "I go to Little Italy."

"Then I can assume you didn't get a call informing you of an auction tonight?"

Giovanni paled.

"I thought so," I said. "Now, here's how we can help each other."

Pausing, I waited to see what other reaction there would be.

Giovanni sighed. "What I do?"

"Tonight, you're going to the auction but are taking two of my companions along."

He smiled.

"And they speak Italian," I added. "By the way, Nǐ huì shuō zhōngwén ma? (Do you speak Chinese?)"

"That no Italian." Giovanni leaned back in his chair. "Sound like Chinese. I no speak it."

I shrugged. "If you do, trust me, I'll be listening and you don't want to know my resolve." I smiled. "Other than nǐ hǎo (hello), I don't want to hear any Chinese coming from this mouth." I stuck my finger between his lips. "Capire? (understand)

He nodded.

"You will attend the auction. You will buy. You can go as high as you want since you really won't be buying any of the girls. And, if you turn state's evidence, you will get off basically Scott-free and your prior indulgences will be exonerated... if you return the merchandise you bought."

Giovanni sighed heavily, glanced in both directions, then nodded agreement.

"Before I forget," I said. "You won't have your henchmen in attendance." I grinned. "No reason to cause a lot of concern, my two men will be the only ones you take. So, what time is the auction?"

A smile spread across Giovanni's face. He shrugged. "I don't know. You have all answers."

I leaned in conspiratorially. "Cooperation is the key here. You don't cooperate and the deal is off." I shrugged. "And, I'll hold you for as long as I see fit." I turned to Willie who stood by the door. "Do you have accommodations for our guest?"

Willie nodded. "A semi-private room with nice stainless-steel toilet and sink, a bunk with a thin mattress... Oh, and a roomie, I think his name is Bubba, about two-hundred seventy-some pounds of pure love machine muscle." Willie hesitated. "I'm told he likes Italian."

Giovanni's eyes widened. "Auction will be at nine tonight at the warehouse on Maple Street. We go in the back."

I had to shake my head with the onslaught of information.

Maple Street? My mind raced. *That's the warehouse across from Bingwen's restaurant.*

"I'll get the paperwork changed," Willie said and left the room.

CHAPTER THIRTEEN

The Auction

I curled up across the street, down about twenty-five feet from Chang's restaurant. My makeshift cardboard bed with newspaper covers I hoped would suffice to create the image of a homeless man. I had considered the alley where all the guests would enter but that was too obvious.

My headset crackled.

"We're going in." It was Antonio Russo, lead on the inside guards of Giovanni Pirozzi. "This is quite some maze," he whispered. "I'm glad Giovanni knows where we're going."

"Keep the line open for listening," Willie said. "Enough chit-chat."

On a whim, I decided to cross the street and enter the warehouse — if the front door was still open. I wadded the newspapers and folded the cardboard, putting it all to the side. I was sure another person would grab that treasure for the night.

I had to act fast since I really didn't want anyone seeing me enter the building and realizing the front door was unlocked.

I fussed with the door, pretending to be unlocking it, opened the door and slipped inside. There was barely any light shining in through the filthy windows of the lobby.

Fortunately, I knew my way to where Zhong had been before, hoping it was the same room he would use for the auction.

I approached the room, there was a light on and I peeked through the same window I had cleaned before.

Five girls sat in chairs with shackles around their ankles with a ball and chain attached. Unfortunately, there was only the girls and three unrecognized men guarding them.

This isn't where the auction is being held, I thought.

In the distance, on down the hall, I heard voices.

This is going to be awkward, I thought. *If I hide in this hallway, when they bring the girls to where the auction is being held, I will be visible.*

A distant door opened and a shadowed body ambled the hallway toward this room and entered.

"Zhang say bring." He grabbed the closest girl and pulled her from the chair. "Move." He leered at her. "Show time." He glared at one of the men. "Get ball and chain removed. Leave shackles."

I didn't know who the girl was, it was one taken last night during the parade. Holly was in the next chair.

Her makeup was almost garish, clownish. Holly was the type of girl who usually wore little, if any makeup. In fact, all the girls had on too much makeup, but that was part of Zhong's plan to sell them.

The ball and chains were removed and the five girls walked from the room in a single file. The four men kept them in line.

I waited in the shadows of the hallway, waiting for them to go into what I could only assume to be the auction room.

"You won't believe who just arrived," Willie said through the headset.

I crept down the hall toward the auction room, carefully cleaning the window to see better into the room.

A tall Chinese gentleman in an off-white linen suit strolled into the room from the other side. I recognized him from Chang's restaurant.

That's Fai Yue, I thought. "Fai Yue," I whispered into my headset.

"How do you know that?" Willie said. There was a pause. "Where are you?"

"Change of plans," I whispered. "I'm inside, staring at the whole auction room."

"Barry!"

I recognized that tone of voice. Willie was more than upset.

"Hush," I said in response. "The auction is about to start."

Fai Yue stepped to the front.

"Welcome, favored buyers." He smiled. "Tonight, we have

five beautiful, young girls for your purchasing pleasure." He waved his hand to encompass the five shackled women. "Two are virgins." Again, he smiled. "They are guaranteed virgin. They were medically checked." Fai took a deep breath. "Unfortunately, not all buyers will be lucky." He paused. "Six buyers, five girls. We will start with..." He turned to face the girls and Zhong moved a girl taken the night before forward. "Ah," Fai said. "Our first virgin of the night." He turned to the group of buyers. "We will start bidding at five grand."

Antonio nudged Giovanni.

"Ten," Giovanni said.

A horn honked, blasting into the silence of the room. Buyers and their guards glanced about the room, nervous, like a deer about to bound away.

Fai gazed around the room. "No need for concern," he said. "My men are above us and if there is a problem, they will eliminate it."

"We just rounded up the drivers and extra henchmen," Willie said. "Sorry about the horn."

"What about the men on top of the building?" I asked.

"Took them out earlier. Had our sharpshooters dart them. They'll sleep for the next hour."

I nodded approval in the darkness of the hallway. I started to count the buyers; I could see five.

Fai Yue thought he had it all under control; little did he know the Blue Lotus Society would be going down tonight.

"Do you know that the Blue Lotus Society is running this show?"

"We did when Fai Yue waltzed in and dispersed his henchmen to the top." There was a smugness in Willie's voice I hadn't noticed before.

"A feather for the cap?" I asked.

"Nope. I'm going for the whole war bonnet," Willie said.

I turned my attention back to the auction.

"Ninety-five." A voice from the shadows to the far right spoke out.

That makes six buyers, I thought, having not seen that particular buyer.

Giovanni sighed. "One hundred."

Fai Yue smiled; he was enjoying the bickering prices of the auction.

"Three hundred fifty." A sheik sitting closest to the stage waved his hand.

"Ah, Sheik Shafiq Awad. *As-Salam 'Alaikum* (hello). You honor us." Fai Yue bowed slightly, placing his hand over his heart in a traditional Arabic greeting.

It was obvious, the auction of this young girl was over and the sheik had the first girl from the auction block.

"Our next delicacy is this young one," Fai Yue said as Zhong moved the girl to the front and under the bright spotlight.

Fai Yue moved to the girl. "As you can see, she is young." He turned to the frightened girl. "How old are you?"

"Twenty-two," the girl whispered.

"Ah, she is twenty-two." Fai glanced out at the audience. "So innocent." He grasped the small bandanna wrapped around her breasts and yanked it away. "Very nubile," he said and touched the left breast. "Soft." He stroked her arm. It was disgusting to watch him paw over her.

The girl attempted to hide her exposed breasts, but Zhong held her arms behind her back.

"One hundred." Again, it was the voice in the back in shadows.

"One hundred twenty-five," Giovanni said.

"One hundred fifty."

I couldn't see who called the amount, he was hidden by a group of men and was sitting in the shadows of the room. *He?* I questioned it; the voice was not the deep, male voice one would expect. At least, it didn't match Giovanni or the sheik

Could it be a woman? I thought.

"Get ready," Willie said. "We're coming in."

I gazed through my peephole and saw our two men with Giovanni nod. They were ready.

To the side and above I heard a soft flapping sound. There had been a hum, but now that was replaced by the soft sound of something repeatedly clicking. I frowned in thought.

CHAPTER FOURTEEN

The Attack

Like the fireworks of the night before, all hell broke loose as men rushed in the back door and from doorway of the hallway. I joined them. The two men with Giovanni pushed him to the ground and held him there; more for his protection than anything else.

Fai Yue grabbed Zhong and pushed him toward the wall. Zhong fumbled his hands on the wall, a small portion slid to the side. Fai Yue pushed Zhong to the floor, stepped into the opening and disappeared from the room.

The secret panel door slid back.

I frowned. Fai Yue was gone. The Blue Lotus Society was off the hook... unless... there was backup outside to nab him.

"Willie," I said into my mouthpiece. "Fai Yue just escaped. You got anybody outside to catch him?"

"We have it covered, Barry."

I shrugged. *Not my worry*, I thought.

Willie and Preston grouped the buyers together. There were six men.

I frowned and gazed about at the collected goons. I counted. Fourteen men, one woman.

Woman? My mind raced. I grabbed Wilie and pulled him to the side.

"I think we are being hook-winked, Willie." I nodded at the buyers. "One of them had a higher voice than the others."

Willie gave me a look like I was crazy. "So?"

"I'm pretty sure all those men you gathered as buyers are deep-voiced. One of the buyers had a higher voice and I think she swapped places with one of her henchmen."

Willie glanced over at the group of thugs. "Hm? Barry, you might be right. Strange to have a woman as a guard, not impossible, but... I'll check into it."

"Hey, Preston," Willie called. "Come here."

Preston ambled over.

"When you check out the henchmen, the woman? Do a thorough on her. Something tells me she was a buyer, not a guard."

"Will do," Preston said. He turned to me. "You want me to call Zimmer about his girlfriend?" He nodded toward Holly who stood huddling with the other girls.

"No need," I said. "I'll take care of it."

Preston nodded and shuffled off toward the group of buyers being led away.

I watched the remaining thugs, the guards; especially the woman. There was a smugness about her. She was cold, but not the typical henchman, guard, or thug type.

What bothered me, she seemed very familiar. I'd seen her somewhere, but I couldn't remember where. *Possibly on the street*, I thought.

#

Outside, I discovered Fai Yue had been captured. There was a stain on his off-white linen suit; a red stain.

Willie walked up to him. "Thought you could get away?"

Fai Yue immediately fell into pigeon English.

"I call lawyer. I out. You no hold me." He placed a hand over his right arm where it bled. "You shoot me. I sue."

Willie got in Fai Yue's face. "First, you speak excellent English so don't give me this pidgin-English crap. In fact, I even heard you speak Arabic." He grinned at Fai Yue. "And it all has been recorded." Willie shrugged. "So, call your lawyer. Do whatever you want. The precinct finally has the goods on you and the Blue Lotus Society." With an index finger thumping Fai Yue on the chest. "Your tong is going down."

Fai Yue sneered. "You prove I was in there. My lawyer prove I wasn't."

"Actually, Fai Yue," I said. "We can prove you were in there. We have pictures. Several, in fact." I turned to Antonio. "How many did you take?"

"At least twenty," Antonio said. "Plus, the recording of his voice during the auction."

Fai Yue paled momentarily. "Not Fai Yue. Somebody else. My lawyer will prove it."

Willie shook his head. "Take him away." Willie turned to me as Fai Yue was led away.

"That's what I fear," he said. "Fai Yue might just get off. His lawyer is good. We just have to make sure all our ducks are lined up and in a perfect row." Willie shook his head and stared down at his shoes. "Yeah, his lawyer will be looking for any crack in our story, even a scratch where he can create a crack." Again, he shook his head. "I just wish we had known where the auction was going to take place so we could have gotten a surveillance camera in."

I frowned. It hit me. "Follow me."

Working my way back to my hiding place in the hallway outside the auction room, I placed a finger to my lips. "Listen."

The flapping sound continued.

Willie reached over and flicked on the light switch. The hallway was flooded in the bright glow of incandescent lights, all the shadows chased away.

To the right, above our heads, we could see the culprit making all the noise.

A camera.

"Son of a..." Willie started. "That's an old eight millimeter camera... and it works!"

"I heard it making that sound just before we broke up the party," I said. "Off hand, I'd say it has the recording of Fai Yue selling the first girl and bringing the second girl up to sell." I slapped Willie on the back. "You have the evidence." I shook my head. "A war bonnet, eh? You got enough feathers collected to have that war bonnet go all the way down to your heels."

Willie laughed. "Of course, you helped."

"Thanks, partner," I replied. "Now, let's get down to the precinct and get things taken care of."

# # #

The precinct was a mess, a chaos of activity. A bust this big hadn't happened for ages, at least two or more years.

Willie walked in and all of the officers, detective, police personnel burst into a thunderous applause and cheering. I saw Willie shrinking in this newfound stardom.

This was his bust, his feather. I patted him on the back. "Enjoy the moment," I whispered and stepped aside so he stood alone.

"A little early to celebrate." The voice yelled above the din. "I'm here for Fai Yue."

I turned to face the voice. Fai Yue's lawyer, none other than Leonard Metzer, stood in the doorway of the precinct.

"I need to see my client," he bellowed.

"You can see your client in due time." Willie was in his moment and wasn't about to give up the limelight just yet. "Currently he is being booked. Once that has been done and all the processes completed, I will personally escort you to the interrogation room for you to discuss matters with your client." He paused. "Understood?"

Leonard Metzer fumed.

"Have a seat, Metzer," Willie said. "Just cool your heels."

"My client has rights," Metzer said. "I can..."

"You can do whatever you wish to do," Willie snapped. "But, until Fai Yue has been processed, you will sit there." Willie pointed at a chair. "Make yourself comfortable."

Willie walked down the hallway toward his office area. I followed. He opened the door and glared at Preston.

"You got Fai Yue. You make sure you cross every "T" and dot every "I" because Fai's lawyer is out there fuming."

Preston looked up and blinked. "I know what to do," he uttered and turned back to his prisoner.

Willie leaned on Preston's desk. "I don't need your crap, Preston. Leonard Metzer doesn't mess around. He'll rip through your report like a shredder." Willie glanced at Fai Yue who sat there smugly smiling. "I don't want this one to slip away."

Fai Yue shrugged. "I'm not the big guy." He grinned. "I am just a pawn in this game. I will be out of here in minutes."

"If you're not the top dog," I started. "Who is?"

I figured it was worth an attempt to see if he'd slip up.

"I'll never tell you her name," he whispered.

I frowned. Her? I thought. Just that fast, I realized we'd not picked up Liang Jin. I turned to Willie.

"Did you get Liang Jin?"

"Yes, I did," Willie replied. "I covered all the tracks." He motioned for me to follow him.

"I didn't want Fai Yue to hear," Willie said as we stood near each other by the doorway. "If he isn't the big cheese, who is?" He frowned at me. "Did you catch that? Her?"

I nodded. I knew what I needed to do. Lian Yoon was my go-to and I hoped he had the answers.

CHAPTER FIFTEEN

Back to Lian

I approached Lian's apartment with some apprehension. I hadn't told Mei and wasn't sure if Lien would talk to me or run. I looked at the door, the hook and eye lock was not connected. I remembered him saying he would talk, but...

Lian is home? I thought.

I knocked and listened for any sound from the other side of the door. There was some shuffling and then I heard somebody approach the door. I hoped it was Lian.

The door cracked.

Lian peeked out.

"Ah, Detective Hargrove," Lian said and opened the door.

I entered and noticed the room hadn't changed much since my last visit. Perhaps newer pizza and Chinese carry out boxes, but otherwise, the room was stagnant.

I ambled across the room and sat on the only chair available. Lian jumped through the air and flopped out on the couch. It groaned in protest.

"Okay, Lian," I started. "You were the tail of the Purple Dragon the other night. Right?"

He nodded.

"Did you realize that the dragon ate two young girls?"

He shrugged. "I saw people leave." He shook his head. "Maybe girls."

I realized the conversation was not getting where I needed.

"Do you know who is in charge of the Purple Dragon?"

"Yes. It Zhong. He hire me."

"No," I replied. "Fai Yue is in charge." I watched Lian.

He shrugged. "I no know him."

"The Blue Lotus Society tong."

His eyes widened. "Blue Lotus? Not good."

I nodded. "Yes, I agree, but I found out he is not the top honcho." I watched Lian. "Do you understand."

"Shì de." (yes) He paused. "I tail, little guy. Zhong, he lower body. Fai Yue, he upper body."

I nodded agreement.

"You want head?" He shrugged. "Who?"

"That's why I'm here, Lian. Do you have any idea who is the head?"

Lian snickered. "Not Zhong. He think he tongue. Wrong." With a grin, he added. "He play tongue."

I couldn't help myself and joined Lian in a laugh. It was ironic.

Suddenly, I realized who the woman was at the auction. It was Lian's neighbor down the hall. And, she was currently being held at the precinct.

Her apartment is open to me, I thought. *Yes, I should have a warrant to search, but...* My mind wrapped around the idea. *I'm a detective. I don't need a warrant.*

"Lian," I started and stood. "I'm going to your neighbor's apartment. You can join me, or not."

Lian stood. I headed for the door and he followed.

"Do you know her name?" I asked Lian as we stood before her door. The hook and eye was engaged, she wasn't home.

Lian shook his head. "She quiet. No talk. Only say 'hello', 'thank you' when I take her garbage out."

I lifted the hook and the door creaked open slightly. I pushed the door with my index finger and it opened all the way.

"Join me?" I asked.

Lian followed me as I walked into the woman's apartment.

The apartment had better amenities, a couch, two chairs, two end tables, a small kitchen table with two chairs. A vase of flowers decorated the table. The apartment was clean. There was a telephone with an answering machine. I rewound the tape and listened.

Ping. Call me. You have the number.

Miss Ping Lin. Tomorrow night, 8:30 p.m., five to auction. Standard location.

I grabbed the answering machine. She may have been able to con one of her henchmen to take her place, but I had the goods. She was going down. She was a buyer.

Nodding to Lian, we headed out the door.

Now, my mind was trying to ascertain if she was another buyer or was she even bigger?

Lian shut the door to his apartment after we'd reentered.

"Detective Hargrove," Lian said. "You take machine. Evidence, yes?"

I nodded.

"No warrant. No good."

Lian was right. Without a proper warrant, the recording would be thrown out of court as evidence. Leonard Metzer would make sure of that.

"Xièxiè," (thank you) I said and headed back to the apartment to replace the machine.

Again, Lian tagged along like a puppy, watching me.

I grabbed the phone in the apartment and called Willie.

"I need a warrant to search an apartment." I gave him the details. "I'll be waiting in Lian's apartment when you arrive."

# # #

An hour later, Willie passed the open door of Lian's apartment. I called to him.

"Here's your warrant," Willie said and passed me the document. "So, what is this for?"

"The woman we have at the precinct from the auction. She lives in that apartment. There is a recording on her answering machine and it is very incriminating. I'm pretty sure she is a buyer, not a guard, goon, or henchman... I mean, henchwoman."

Once more we ambled to Miss Lin's apartment where I rewound the tape to play for Willie.

... so you can see the new sofa. Call me.

Miss Lin, Fai Yue here. All is arranged per your instructions.

Call me. You have the number

Miss Ping Lin. Tomorrow night, 8:30 p.m., five to auction. Standard location.

"I think we found our big cheese," I said. "I only knew Yue had called. I rewound further this time. Lucky us."

"Let me call the precinct. Rumor is the guards will be released." He picked up the phone and dialed.

"Preston." Willie rolled his eyes and shook his head. "Listen. You make sure that both Fai Yue and Miss Ping Lin are kept overnight. They are not, I repeat, NOT to be released."

Willie hung up the phone. "I hope that jerk does what I told him. He always thinks his way is the best."

"Well, then, I'd suggest we get back to the precinct and protect our investments."

I turned to Lian. "Again, thank you."

Lian grinned. "Maybe I become private detective, too." He stepped into his apartment. "Better job. Honest."

CHAPTER SIXTEEN

Ping Lin

I followed Willie into the 'Missing Persons' office. Preston sat his desk, making paper airplanes and sailing them across the room.

"What cell did you put Miss Ping Lin..."

Preston's look stopped Willie in mid-sentence.

"Metzer said we had no grounds for holding his clients." He plopped his feet up on the desk, leaning back in his chair.

I watched Willie. He stood there, drawing in a deep breath, an almost insusceptible shaking. He clenched his hands into fists.

"Did I not tell you to keep her?" Willie's voice was low and monotone.

"Well, Leonard Metzer gave me two choices. Either I released Fai Yue and Ping Lin, or I could start looking for a new job."

Willie shook his head. "You believed him?" He grabbed a chair and sat. "Plug that damned thing in, Barry. Let our fool here listen to what it offers."

I plugged the answering machine in and rewound it a bit. I hit play and we listened to the messages.

"Did you hear that?" Willie asked as he glared at Preston. "Fai Yue is a pawn... maybe a knight or bishop in this game, but Miss Lin is our queen." He inhaled. "And, you let her go."

"How was I to know?" Preston dropped his feet to the floor.

"Hm?" Willie leaned in toward Preston. "Maybe because I said to hold them and not let them go, no matter what."

Preston, once more, leaned back in his chair and shrugged

with unconcern. "Well, they're gone."

"Like the queen on a chessboard, Miss Lin can move anywhere she desires." Willie slapped his open hand on Preston's desk. "Because of you, our main suspect is gone."

"Maybe yes, maybe no," I said. "Get some squad cars over to her apartment. Now!"

Willie nodded and Preston grabbed the phone and expedited the request.

"I figure she has skipped," I said. "Still, there is a chance she might have gone back to her apartment." I had an idea. "I'll be right back."

Moving to Willie's desk, I grabbed the phone and called Chang's Restaurant.

"Hey, Bingwen," I said as he answered the phone. "Is Mei working tonight?" A pause. "She is? Can I speak with her; it's sort of important."

Mei picked up the phone. "*Nǐ hǎo*, (hello) Detective Hargrove."

"Hi, Mei. Do you have a way to contact your cousin, Lian? I mean, like a phone number?"

"Sometime he has cell phone. I can call." Mei's voice was meek.

"Can you give me the number?" I wasn't sure Mei could hear my urgency. "I need to contact him right now."

"His number 555-4972."

"Local area code?" I asked and could almost hear Mei nod.

"Yes," she replied.

"Thank you," I said and hung up, immediately dialing Lian's phone, hoping it worked.

"*Nǐhǎo*," (hello") Lian answered.

"Lian," I said. "This is Detective Hargrove. I need you to do some detective work for me. Is Miss Ping Lin in her apartment, and if so, can you keep her there until the police arrive?"

I heard Lian's door creak open.

"She there," he whispered. "How I keep her?"

"Grab a bag and put some garbage in it then go ask her if she has any. Just keep her there. If you want, ask her if she enjoyed the

Lantern Festival."

"I try." He hung up.

I stood and walked over to Preston's desk where Willie and he were talking.

"Let's go," I said to Willie. "I got Lian keeping Miss Lin occupied." I shrugged. "We may have lost Fai Yue, but I'm more interested in getting her."

I started out of the office, unsure if Willie was following, or not. I just hoped Preston kept his butt in his chair.

Stepping into the hallway, Willie caught up with me. Preston was still in his chair.

CHAPTER SEVENTEEN

Standoff

We arrived at Lian's apartment building. All the flashing lights; there had to be at least twenty-five squad cars positioned around the building. Police were at their ready, guns pulled and aimed at the third floor. There was no way Ping Lin was getting away.

Willie led the way into the building, cutting a path for us through all the police. He entered the building and I showed him the way up the stairs. This time I knew I wanted to have my breath when I arrived at the top, so I moved cautiously up the stairs, gun drawn, sliding against the wall to keep an eye on the above scenario.

Nothing happened.

Lian's apartment door was open as we passed it. Willie gave it a quick scan with his eyes and gun. Nothing.

In front of us, at the end of the hallway, three police officers stood before an open door, their guns pulled and aimed.

Willie slid in beside one of the officers.

"Lian?" I called. "You in there?"

"Yes. I..." The voice choked off.

"Are you okay?"

A choked yes was the reply. I couldn't see anything so I gallantly moved between Willie and the door.

Lian was in a chair, tied, hands behind his back, and each foot tied to a leg of the chair.

Beside him stood Ping Lin. She held a *kila*. I gazed at the distant wall, a shadow of where it had hung was all that showed.

My mind raced, I knew it to be a *kila*, a ceremonial wooden dagger of ancient India that found its way to Tibet and Buddhist monasteries and was called a *phurba*. Ping's hand wrapped around the handle, but the tip of it still showed and I saw the wrathful deity known as Vajrakilaya whose three faces showed. I frowned. What she held was wood, not really a weapon to be used on another human with its three-edged blade, again, wood.

Kila (to left)

Sacrificial knife blade (above)

Once more I glanced up the wall where the *kila* had hung. I spied an ancient green-patina bronze Chinese sacrificial knife blade. It lacked a handle, but still, the serrated edge revealed what I considered a keen edge, even after all these years since it was 12th century BC.

If Ping Lin truly planned to slit Lian's throat, the *kila* was not the instrument of death. Even if Ping decided to impale the kila into Lian's neck, the amount of muscle required I felt was beyond her ability. Yes, Lian would hurt, but I truly didn't think the kila would break the skin.

Can I take that chance? I thought.

Lian's eyes revealed what I needed to know. He was terrified. *Does he still want to be a detective?* I wondered.

I turned my attention to Ping Lin. I shook my head.

"Ping Lin," I started. "You were arrested and booked with the intent to purchase illegal goods..." I shrugged. "Or something to that fact. Right now you're facing additional charges; an attempt to flee and jump bond, probably out of the country, possible kidnapping, hostage abuse, intent to kill. I tell you, Ping, you're ringing up charges faster than a pinball machine."

Willie snorted in laughter behind me. "Nice one," he whispered.

"You come closer, I push in Lian's throat."

I saw Lian wince as the *kila* tightened against his neck.

Like a bolt of lightning, I remembered Lian knew sign language.

I signed. *See foot? Stomp. Use chair.*

"Why you move hands?" Ping Lin asked.

In answer, Lian leaned back, lifted the chair leg up, swiveled it, and came down on Ping's foot.

The ensuing scream reverberated within the room. It was high pitched.

Ping Lin dropped the *kila* and it clattered to the floor.

Again, I signed: *tip over, knock her.*

Lian frowned and attempted to shrug.

I tried again: *tip over.*

He nodded.

I signed: *hit her.*

Lian leaned as much as he could to tip the chair over. It hesitated, then the one side of legs lifted and Lian was tumbling toward Ping Lin. He hit her with the chair and his shoulder, catching her so she crumbled like a broken cookie.

The look of shock on her face told me everything. She literally had no idea what hit her.

I raced in to help Lian sit back up. I dropped down and began to untie his feet. Turning slightly, I saw Willie holding Ping Lin down and slapping cuffs on her.

"You have the right..."

The Miranda mantra began and Ping Lin squirmed, attempting to escape.

"This time, Miss Lin, you're going to get a nice cell until the judge decides what to do with you." He glanced over to the phone on the small table. "Notice the answering machine is gone?" He nodded. "Yes, evidence."

Once more Ping Lin struggled to set herself free.

Willie helped her to her feet. "Don't bother running," he said. "We have the building surrounded and there are at least twenty or so squad cars outside." He let her go. "If you want to run, be my guest. I only know of one person who is faster than a speeding bullet, and trust me, Miss Lin, it isn't you." He grinned.

"You still want to be a detective?" I asked Lian.

He shook his head. "You teach me?"

I shrugged. "We'll see."

CHAPTER EIGHTEEN

The Precinct

Preston sat in his chair, leaning back, feet on the desk, arms behind his head, relaxing.

"Hey, Preston," Willie said as he walked into the office. "Do me a favor." He pushed Ping Ling toward him. "Book her then assign her a cell. She won't be going anywhere this time."

Preston sat up. "What do I book her for?"

Willie shrugged. Open the book, point to a law, use it." He grinned. "Okay, use human trafficking, intent to kill, taking a hostage, and the possibility of bail flight..." He made a face. "Guess that could be for starters."

"I get phone call," Ping Lin said.

Willie headed for his desk.

"I say I get phone call." Ping repeated.

"I heard you," Willie replied. "Let me guess... hm? Nope! Not him." Willie grinned as he paused. "Let me try, again. Hm? Nope, not her, either. Third guess. Okay, I'm guessing Leonard Metzer." He picked up the phone and dialed the lawyer's number. "Preston, give her the phone, it's ringing."

Ping Lin glared at Willie but took the phone from Preston.

"You come," she yelled into the phone. "I in jail, again. I want out, now!" She slammed the phone down on the receiver.

Preston glared at her. "That's not your phone," he said softly. "Police property. Treat it respectfully."

Ping Lin turned away and waved her hand to dismiss him.

"It's not that easy," Preston said. "Let's see what we have here." He pulled out a report sheet. "Ah, yes, this is the original one that I was supposed to get rid of when you were released." He grinned at her. "Good thing I decided to keep it..." He paused. "For prosperity."

Ping Lin turned and faced Preston. "You not funny."

"I'm a lot funnier than you," Preston replied. "Now, let's see what I need to update this report. My. My."

Willie sat his desk and I sat opposite him. He was looking at the different reports, always coming back to the one with Fai Yue's name on it.

"What's the problem?" I asked.

"I'm trying to figure out where Fai Yue would go to hide." He moved the sheets around. "Zhong is in a cell downstairs. Who would think to look at his place?"

I cocked an eye at Willie. "Obviously, you would. Ready to go?"

Willie nodded, stood and headed for the door. He stopped and turned to face Preston.

"This time, you make sure she gets her accommodations. She has reservations." Willie grabbed the doorknob. "Oh, when her lawyer, Leonard Metzer shows up. Don't take any crap or threats. She is being booked and held. No release. Understood?"

Preston nodded. "Got it."

I followed Willie out the door and down the hall of the precinct. A few quick steps and we were in Willie's car headed for Zhong's apartment... and, hopefully, Fai Yue.

We climbed the stairs of the rickety building. I kept an eye open for anything unusual, but everything seemed a little unusual in this building. I grinned.

At least it isn't like Lian's building; the doors have actual locks, I thought.

"Do we knock?" Willie asked. "I mean, he's in jail, but I didn't really check his sheet. Was he married? Family?"

"Knock," I said. "If somebody answers, we'll go from there."

Willie slammed his hand against the door three times. "Police."

That's being subtle, I thought.

Willie waited; I could tell he was counting.

"Nobody home," he said and tried the doorknob.

It turned and we entered Zhong's apartment.

I gazed about the room; definitely a bachelor lived here. A couch, two chairs, a couple of tables with lamps, a kitchen table with four chairs, and empty food cartons everywhere. A doorway led to the bedroom; a mattress on the floor, clothes strewn about, some dangling on a lone chair, most were on the floor.

"What are you looking for?" Willie asked.

I shrugged. *What am I looking for?* The words echoed in my mind. *Anything that looks out of place.*

Gazing at the two rooms, everything looked out of place. Another door led to a bathroom. I peeked in.

The shower curtain moved. I waited. It moved again. I reached over and pulled the curtain back; revealing a claw tub and an open window which was the culprit.

The crystal on my watch flashed. I frowned. Gazing at the window, I assured myself it was too small for almost anyone, except possibly a very small child, to escape through.

I stepped back and closed the bathroom door.

"See anything?" Willie asked.

I nodded and placed a finger to my lips. "Fai Yue, I think," I whispered.

"What? And you let him go?"

I shook my head. "No. He's hiding in the tub, behind the shower curtain. I think he was going to try and escape out the window but it is too small." I shrugged. "For the time being, he is a prisoner in the bathroom."

"I'll get reinforcements," Willie said and called the precinct, requesting backup.

CHAPTER NINETEEN

Fai Yue

Five officers entered Zhong's apartment. Willie nodded approval and strolled to the bathroom door.

Rapping on the door with his knuckle, he waited. There was no response.

"Fai Yue," Willie called. "We know you are in there and have no escape. Come out."

A rustling from inside the bathroom confused Willie.

"What is he doing?" Willie asked.

"I'm guessing he's attempting to escape out the window." I rolled my eyes. "Go ahead, open the door and see what's happening."

"Detective Williamson," the walkie-talkie squelched. "Sergeant Miller here. Do you realize there is a man attempting to climb out the window on the fourth floor?"

Willie shook his head. "This should be good." He turned the doorknob. "Coming in."

He was greeted with the backside of Fai Yue hanging from the small window. One arm and head were outside, but the rest of the body remained on this side, completely stuck in the window. Fai Yue could not move forward, nor could he move back.

"Sergeant," Willie called. "Bring in your men. We need to free Fai Yue from the window."

Four officers crowded into the small bathroom and immediately snickered.

"This is going to take some time," the sergeant said. "We might need to call the fire department to assist." He nodded toward the backside of Fai Yue. "We are up four stories. Not the easiest work area." He shrugged. "Ain't no balcony on the other side, either."

"Get me out," Fai Yue screamed.

"In time," Willie replied. "In time. You got yourself in this mess, we're working to get you out." He giggled. "I wouldn't be in a big rush Fai Yue. Remember, when you get free, you're not really free. You're going to jail."

"I don't care; get me out!"

"Can you answer a few questions, Fai Yue?" I asked.

"No."

"You're the leader of the Blue Lotus Society tong. True?"

"Yes."

"Who is is the leader of the young girl kidnapping ring?"

Silence.

"Oh, look, Willie," I said. "It appears they've brought in a jackhammer to break the wall."

"No," Fai Yue yelled.

"Hold it, boys," I said. There was nobody, but Fai Yue couldn't see that.

"Who is the leader?" I asked, again.

"Liang Jin. He holds the girls," Fai Yue said.

"Yes, I know that, but he isn't the leader."

"I only auction the girls," Fai Yue said.

"And I know that, too, but again, you're not the big cheese. Who is it?" I placed the shaver against the window's frame and turned it on.

"I don't know her name," Fai Yue said.

"Yet, you called her." I paused. "So, let me get this straight. You pick up the phone, dial some random number, and she picks up. Is that correct?"

"Yes, I made the call. I called her." The voice was frantic. "Please, no jackhammer."

I turned off the shaver; amazed Fai Yue thought it to be a jackhammer. *Is he in for a surprise when they do show up with a jackhammer or a saws-all*, I thought.

"If I remember correctly, you called and said 'Miss Lin' during the call." I paused for the information to soak in. "Therefore, you knew who you were calling. Is that not correct?"

"Yes. Yes." Fai Yue squirmed, trying to get free. "I know her, the name is Ping Lin and she's my boss for the auctions."

"And, yet she pretended to be a buyer?" I asked.

"Oh, she is a buyer," Fai Yue said. "She wants a girl for..."

Willie leaned in. "Speak up, Fai Yue. We didn't hear the end of that sentence."

"I didn't finish the sentence," Fai Yue croaked as he again attempted to move backwards out of the window. "She likes girls."

"Are you saying Miss Lin is...?" I left the sentence unfinished.

"No, she's not that. She wants girl slaves to wait on her."

I heard the sirens of the firetrucks approaching.

"You'll be free soon," I said. "How much of the cut do you get?"

Fai Yue grunted and I could see his contortions in his feeble attempts to free himself.

"I asked a question. Wait. Hold still," I said. "The fireman is here to get you free."

A man with a saws-all running full-tilt approached the window.

"I'll have you out in no time," he said and applied the saw to the edge of window, breaking through the frame and wall to open the area.

Fai Yue wiggled.

"Hold still and you won't get cut," the fireman said as the saw crawled up the wall, opening even more space.

"Now," the fireman said and pulled Fai Yue by the belt around his waist.

Fai Yue fell backwards from the opening and into the tub.

"I'm free," Fai Yue said.

"Not really. You're under arrest," Willie countered and pulled cuffs out and let them swing in the air. "Hands out."

Fai Yue offered his two hands and Willie snapped the cuffs on.

"Let's get you back to the precinct," Willie said. "This time you can call Leonard Metzer, but you're not being set free."

Fai Yue nodded.

CHAPTER TWENTY

Loose Ends

I sat quietly in the car as Willie drove us back to the station.

Something isn't right, I thought. It hit me. *We saved these girls, but what of the others? Where are they?*

Willie gazed at me. "I'd say a penny for your thoughts, but you'd share and expect me to pay up."

"No penny required," I said. "We saved these five girls, but what of the others? Where are they? How do we get them back?"

"That's a pretty hefty thought," Willie said. There was a pause. "And I figure you have an answer."

I shrugged in the darkness of the car. "Not really and that's what bothering me."

Willie snorted in laughter. "Barry Hargrove. Detective Barry Hargrove lost for words. No plan." He shook his head. "I never thought I'd live to see this day come."

"Oh, trust me, my old partner. Something will come to me. I just need time."

"Uh-huh," Willie mumbled. "We're here so let's get Fai Yue and Ping Lin put away this time." He got out of the car, leaned over the top of it to face me. "I just realized; Fai Yue is the leader of the Blue Lotus Society. With him behind bars, that tong may fall apart now."

I shook my head. "Not really, Willie," I replied. "They probably already have a new tong leader. We just need to be observant and figure out who is next in line, or has the guts to take the job." I smiled. "The Blue Lotus Society tong will exist long after we're gone."

Willie sighed, stepped back, and closed the car door.

#

We walked into the office and Preston immediately sat up in his chair.

"Uh, when I was locking up Ping Lin downstairs. I had two women guards assist me so there wasn't any possibility of Ping Lin using some sexual harassment crap coming up later and she'd get free. Anyway, Shafiq Awad wanted to talk to you." He shrugged. "Wouldn't talk to me; said he wanted the man in charge." He stared at Willie. "I'm guessing that is you."

"I'll have him brought up," Willie said and turned to me. "What do you think he wants?" He picked up the phone and called lockup.

"We'll know shortly," I said and sat in the chair at the side of Willie's desk. "Maybe I should be on my way. I need to let James Zimmer know Holly Brockwood has been found."

"I called him," Preston said, rather proud of himself. "I knew you were busy, so I did it. When I asked if he'd been notified, he said he hadn't heard anything."

"Thanks," I replied, slightly miffed the grand moment of achievement had been taken away. *Zimmer should stop by the office and we'll finalize the bill*, I thought.

"Ah, the sheik is here," Willie said noticing the door opening and Shafiq Awad and two guards coming into the room.

I got up to allow the sheik a place to sit and talk with Willie.

"Detective Hargrove," the sheik said. "Can we make a deal?"

I was flabbergasted. He should have been talking to Willie.

"What kind of deal?" Willie asked, taking control of the situation. "Detective Hargrove is a private investigator and not part of the police precinct."

"I want to be set free. I..." He gazed about the room, noting Fai Yue. "Can we talk elsewhere?"

Willie stood. "Follow me." He started out the door; Shaliq Awad followed with his two guards. I followed, hoping I would be allowed to be part of the conference.

Opening a door, Willie stepped aside. "We can talk in here." He motioned for the two guards to wait outside.

I boldly strode into the room.

"I shouldn't allow it," Willie whispered as I passed him. "But, you've been instrumental in this case." He motioned for me continue into the room.

"Have a seat, sheik."

Shaliq Awad took a seat at the table and Willie sat opposite him. I stood in the shadows by the door.

"So you want to be free," Willie said.

"That and I promise never to step on U. S. soil again."

"Well, it depends on what you have to offer," Willie mumbled. "Spill it."

"Ping Lin is in charge." Shaliq Awad's words were delivered with no remorse.

"We already know that," Willie said. "So, no deal." Willie moved to stand from the chair.

"Wait," Shaliq Awad said. "She has an office, and there is a book."

That caught my attention; I moved closer.

"Book?" Willie repeated. "Where is this office?"

"It's off an alley, and has a fake lock door." Shaliq Awad grinned. "Now, do I get a deal?"

"What is in the book?" I asked.

"How much each girl sold for and to who."

Willie eased back into his chair. "A deal, eh?" He cast a glance of indifference at me then looked back to Shaliq. "I could be persuaded if... IF the book does, indeed, exist."

"I saw book last time I was at auction. I bought..." Shaliq Awad hesitated. "I bought three girls last time."

I braced myself on the table, my knees trying to give out. "Three?" I whispered.

Shaliq Awad nodded. "I get three. Giovanni Pirozzi, he get one." He paused in thought. "Nine girls sold that night."

"Nine?" Willie sputtered. "When was this?"

"Last year." Shaliq frowned. "Maybe late November?"

Willie leaned in across the table. "I'll make you a deal. You get to go free with a few stipulations. One, you show us this book. Two, you never come back to the United States of America. Three, you return... I am hoping all the girls you bought are still alive." He scowled at Shaliq who nodded. "All the girls you've bought."

Shaliq shrugged. "What if girls want to stay with me? They are free in my home. None have run away."

Willie paused in thought. "If they wish to stay with you, I'm not going to force them back. If a missing person report has their name on it, they need to get in contact with the person who reported it." Willie stared into Shaiq's eyes. "Do you agree?"

Shaliq Awad nodded. "I agree." He lifted his hands, wanting the cuffs removed from his wrists.

"Not so fast," Willie said. "Once we have the book, then, and only then will I remove your bracelets. Understood?"

Shaliq slumped back into his chair, his hands dropping into his lap. He nodded.

"Okay, now let's get to this office. We'll take a squad car. But, first, we go back to my office so I can get the proper paperwork. I don't want Ping Lin getting off on a technicality." Willie stood. "Do you wish to sit here and wait, or come to my office?"

"I sit here," Shaliq Awad said. "I have no desire to see Fai Yue."

"Your call, sheik," Willie said. "I'll have a guard in here and another outside the door."

Shaliq Awad glared at Willie.

"For your protection, sheik," Willie told him. "For your protection."

CHAPTER TWENTY-ONE

Ping's Office

Shaliq Awad spilled the address as we drove to where I figured we were headed. The alley was empty, even the dumpster was missing. That made me a little suspicious. As the headlights of the squad car hit the door, it was obvious the door hadn't been put back to appear locked.

"Not good," Willie said, parking the squad car. "You're sure this is right place?"

"Yes, it is," Shaliq Awad said. "We go in, take a left, go about three doors. Ping Lin's office is on the right."

I tried to remember the path we'd taken that night; similar but different. I pushed the door open. Darkness greeted us.

"Light to left on the wall," Shaliq said.

I flipped the switch and an incandescent glowed filled the hallway.

In the distance, scrambling sounds as one or more persons attempted to escape.

Willie pulled his gun and slammed up against the wall, pushing Shaliq beside him.

I cautiously moved forward, keeping down so I was below most of the windows lining the hallway.

The room where Zhong had kept the girls prior to the auction was bright. In the far distance, at the opposite wall, I heard indistinct voices as they fought with each other.

I stepped into the room. Brooms and mops lay helter-skelter

on the floor. Partially filled boxes of paper and other trash were scattered about. The smell of bleach and peroxide hung in the air.

They were cleaning this place, I thought, not trying to be obvious. *But, who?*

When I turned to face my companions, I expected to see Willie, but didn't. Shaliq placed a finger to his lips. I frowned.

Once more, scuffling on the opposite side of the big room caught my attention.

Willie's voice rumbled across the open space. "Hands up. Stand still."

Three men lumbered from the darkness of the other side. Behind them was Willie.

"They tried and almost got away," he said, wielding his gun to direct them into the center of the room.

I grabbed Shaliq by his loose kurta shirt as he attempted to slip away.

"Not so fast or you're going to lose your deal," I whispered.

Shaliq, still in cuffs, ambled into the middle of the room with the other three men.

"What was going on here?" Willie asked.

Each of the three looked back and forth at each other, finally all three looking at Shaliq.

"Don't look at me," Shaliq said, shaking his head. "I have no idea what was going on."

One stepped forward, a thin Chinese man.

"We clean room. Zhong tell us two day ago." He looked at Willie, me, then Shaliq.

"Why do you all keep staring at the sheik?" I asked.

The one who had been speaking motioned for me to come closer. I hesitated on his request, but decided to toss caution to the side. I leaned in.

"He not sheik," the man said. "He Ping Lin old boyfriend before Fai Yue." He giggled. "I think Ping Lin find out he not real sheik, dump him. She want power man like Fai Yue."

I scowled at the man. "Are you sure?"

He nodded his head.

"How do you know this?" My curiosity was totally piqued.

"Are you two about finished?" Willie asked.

"Give me a couple more minutes," I replied.

Shaliq Awad real name, but not sheik. He kitchen help Golden China buffet." He looked me straight in the eye. "I work buffet, too. I also body of Green Dragon." He tapped his chest with his index finger proudly then glared at Shaliq. "He work Purple Dragon, no honor."

That caught me off-guard, but decided I would get back to it later, if needed.

"How do you know Zhong?"

"He work Hong Kong Export next door buffet. He pay me clean room. I get brother and cousin help."

I noticed Willie getting antsy. I held up my index finger to indicate a moment longer.

"So what do you clean?"

"This room, hallway. Use bleach. No stain allowed. Zhong very clear, no stain."

"Did Zhong already pay you?"

He nodded.

"Good. Go home. You're free." I started to walk away, and turned back to the threesome. "Don't work for Zhong anymore."

The three of them shook their heads. "No Zhong."

"What are you doing," Willie yelled. "You let them go."

"They're here to clean up any evidence. Want them to continue?"

Willie offered me a sheepish smile. "Uh, no. But we could have arrested them for tampering with evidence."

I turned to Shaliq Awad. "Okay, now where is this office with the book?"

Shaliq Awad gazed at me, momentarily frowning, unsure.

I knew he wanted to know what transpired between the cleaning guy and me. I wasn't about to reveal that information, just yet.

He led us out of the big room, back into the hallway and to the office he had told us about. I flicked on the light and a sole desk and two chairs were the only things there. One chair was behind the desk, the other was in front.

I could see Ping Lin doing business. She struck me as very to-the-point without a lot of extra fluff.

"Where's the book?" I asked.

Shaliq Awad motioned to the left. "Top drawer under fake bottom."

Willie held Shaliq and I moved to the chair, sat, and opened the top left drawer. Pushing papers back, I found the release for the fake bottom. If I'd not known, I would not have noticed it. The bottom flipped up and there it was; the book.

"It's here," I said and plopped it on the desk which, to my surprise, was not dusty, but clean.

I opened the book and noted the numbers, the only thing I could read. The rest was in Chinese.

"We need an interpreter," I said and held the book for Willie to see.

"Bingwen?" Willie asked.

I nodded.

"Oh, by the way..." I started. "Take our so-called sheik back to the jail. His deal is off. Not exactly sure how he planned to not be on our country's land since he works at the Golden Gate buffet, but..."

"He what?" Willie asked.

"Our sheik is not a sheik but an old boyfriend of Ping Lin. You take our 'sheik' back to jail and meet me at Chang's."

"Okay, but you don't start without me," Willie said. "I want to know what is in that book, too."

I nodded.

CHAPTER TWENTY-TWO

Chang's Again

I walked into Chang's and was immediately greeted by Bingwen.

"Ah, Detective Hargrove." Bingwen glanced at his watch. "It is early for a meal."

"Not looking for food, but, well, maybe an eggroll and some tea. Willie will be here shortly." I nodded at my favorite booth. "Over there?" I asked.

Bingwen nodded and shouted Chinese at the the kitchen. Mei stuck her head out and nodded, then disappeared.

"I need you to look and translate a book we found," I said as I sat at the booth.

I held the book and Bingwen sat down, watching me intently. Finally, he opened his hands on the table top. "Am I to read the book without opening it?"

Grinning, I shook my head. "When Willie gets here; he wants to be a part of the process."

Bingwen frowned but leaned back in the booth. "I understand."

Mei appeared with two cups, a teapot, and a pile of eggrolls.

"Another cup," I said. "Willie will be here shortly."

On cue, he appeared at the back of the restaurant, using the rear door to make his entrance. Willie slid in beside me and I laid the book on the table to slide over to Bingwen.

"This is a book that Ping Lin supposedly kept of all the transactions of the auctions," Willie said. "We can read the numeric amounts, but everything else is in Chinese." He shrugged. "Can you help?"

Bingwen took the book and opened it to the first page. His

fingers glided across the page.

"Old. This date three years ago. Amount is..." He frowned. "Three hundred fifty thousand. Name say Jessie." He looked up from the book and gazed at us.

"Okay," Willie said. "Looks like I've got my work cut out for me." He tapped the book. "Does it say any other name?"

Bingwen glanced at the book. "It says Argus Myles." He leaned back in the booth. "Who is Argus Myles?"

"From what we can tell, Bingwen," I said. "Jessie was sold to Argus three years ago for that amount?"

"Sold?" Bingwen's eyes widened. "Who is peddling flesh in Chinatown?"

I shrugged. "From what we can tell, Ping Lin. We've got a little story editing to do to get all the facts, but go to the last few entries. Who were the buyers and names of the girls sold?"

Bingwen flipped through the pages to the last page with writing.

"There are five names, no other information other than the date of two days ago. The names are Misty, Helen, Holly, Myra, and Barbara."

I nodded. "Those were the last five from the auction the other night." I nodded at the book. "The others?"

Bingwen passed his hand across the page.

"Two hundred sixty-seven thousand. Jackie. Giovanni Pirozzi. November 30."

He read the next line.

"One hundred ninety thousand. Gloria. Argus Myles again. November 30."

His hand slid to the next entry.

"Three hundred thousand. Mary. Peter Gunther. Again, November 30."

I scribbled down the names, amounts, buyers, and dates, hoping I could match some of the files I had at the office.

"Ninety thousand. Inez. Peter Gunther, but on September 18."

"How much?" Willie asked.

"Ninety thousand," Bingwen repeated and frowned. "So little?"

Willie leaned back in the booth. "Inez. Inez." He shook his head. I don't recognize the name."

"The name is of Hispanic origins," I said. "Is it possible she was an illegal immigrant?"

Willie shrugged. "That could explain why there was no missing person report."

I grabbed the book and counted the number of girls that had been sold. The number was staggering. I dropped the book on the table, leaned back, and shook my head.

"Over one hundred," I whispered in a mumble.

"We don't have that many missing reports," Willie said.

Bingwen took the book and looked at us. "Should I continue?"

I nodded and began to write as he translated, but after another fifteen names, I motioned for him to stop.

"If we need more names, I'll be back." I grabbed my tea and sucked it down.

"Holy crap!" Willie exclaimed. "This is tea; not some backyard swill. You savor the flavor."

He did exactly what I hoped he wouldn't. He lifted his teacup to his lips... and slurped.

I cringed. Glancing at Bingwen, I could see him shiver as a chill ran down his back, but he revealed nothing.

"Mr. Williamson certainly enjoys his tea." Bingwen stood. "I must get back to work now. You don't need me anymore, do you?"

"Xiexie," (thank you) I said, stood and gave a small bow.

Willie grabbed the book. "Did you hear the numbers? The dollars? Ping Lin must have millions stashed somewhere."

I shrugged. "Maybe. She had a lot of overhead. Two warehouses, plus Jin's candy shop." I paused. *Why was Liang Jin involved? What did he get out of the deal?*

"You still got Liang Jin in jail?" I asked.

Willie nodded. "Why?"

"Unsure right now," I replied. "Just trying to figure all this out. Exactly what did Liang get out of the deal?"

"Let's go ask," Willie said and got up from the booth. He turned and grabbed the teapot. I put my hand on the pot and held it to the table.

"No," I said. "Let's go." I moved him toward the back door

and his vehicle.

CHAPTER TWENTY-THREE

Questioning

"I need to stop by the office," I said.

Willie pulled up to the curb. "Hurry back," he said.

I rushed up the steps and into the building, pulling my keys out as I headed to the office. Unlocking the door, leaving the keys in the lock, I pushed the door open and raced to the desk. Almost pulling the drawer with the file of missing girls from the desk, I grabbed the file folder and rushed back to the door, locked it, and headed out.

# # #

"Okay, Liang," I said. "I'm trying to figure things out and I don't exactly see where you come into the equation. What do you get out of this auction business?"

Liang sighed. "Baba (father) thinks he sells much candy. Not true. I get money to hold girls. Baba not know. He think we make much money. He sell maybe fifty, sixty dollar of Dragon Beard each day." Liang shook his head. "Not enough pay rent. Zhong pay me money to hold girls. I feed them. Baba no go down to basement."

I nodded. "So, basically, you're subsidizing your father's business. You're keeping him happy in his old age."

Liang nodded. "He happy man, sitting in window, making Dragon Beard."

"As I understand now, you are the holding tank, per se, until the auction. Is that correct?"

Again, Liang nodded. "I bring shame on family."

I glanced around the precinct. There wasn't any sword around. The last time I heard those words, Chen's daughter impaled herself on a Jian sword.

"Don't go committing suicide," I said. "I'm not sure exactly how much shame you've brought on your family." I hesitated and looked at Willie. "I think we might be able to let you go and have you show up when all this goes to court."

Liang's eyes filled with hope. "Baba worry. I go home?"

Willie shrugged. "Sure, why not? I mean, you were involved, but we got the real culprits. You might do some time, but I think we can work something out." He stood. "I'll go start the paperwork."

"Now, first thing, Liang. You must figure out a way to bring in more money." I paused. "Could you get Baba to teach others how to make Dragon Beard?"

Liang nodded. "That help, maybe."

I strode over to Willie's desk. "Can I get Giovanni up here? I want to find out about his last purchase."

Willie glanced at Preston who twiddled a pencil in his hand.

"Can you get Giovanni Pirozzi up here?"

"Sure," Preston said and grabbed the phone. "Bring Giovanni Pirozzi up." He hung up the phone. "Be here in a few minutes."

I was not impressed; neither was Willie.

"Thanks for all the work, Preston," Willie said, the sarcasm lost on Preston.

Giovanni strolled into the room with a guard on each side, his hands in cuffs.

Willie waved a hand to dismiss the guards.

"I got him," Willie said.

"Now, Giovanni," I started. "Exactly what did you do with your last purchase..." I grabbed my notebook. "Ah, yes, two hundred sixty-seven thousand dollars. A Miss Jackie. On November 30, last year."

Giovanni winced.

"Do you want to get back on your plane and fly to Italy?" I asked.

Giovanni nodded. "Yes, of course. I helped you; I get let go."

"Yes, you helped, but this isn't your first rodeo, big boy. You've been to the auction more than once."

Giovanni shrugged to dismiss the accusation.

"What is the status of Miss Jackie?" I asked again.

He squirmed in the chair. "She work my house. I feed her, dress her. She lucky girl."

"Exactly what type of work does Miss Jackie do?" I pressed.

"She meet my friends. She party."

"Uh-huh," I mumbled. "Party girl, eh?"

"Yes. Yes. Party girl." Giovanni came alive. "She party girl. All like her."

"Are you willing to give her back?" I asked.

Giovanni eyes widened. "Back? She like me. She like Italy. She happy."

"Can I ask her that?"

"How?" Giovanni was gallant in his question.

I gazed at Willie who shrugged.

"We have two choices. You fly her to us so we can ask. Or, I go to Italy and I ask for myself."

Giovanni eased back into the chair, not quite so arrogant. "I will fly her here." His eyes brightened. "Tonight? I take plane and fly to Italy and return."

Willie strode over and patted Giovanni on the back, giving him a short massage. "Sure thing, old chap. We'll just let you free to go to Italy and we never see you or Jackie again." He shook his head. "I don't think so, but nice try."

"I have plane fly her to you," he said, the wind definitely knocked from his sails.

Willie sat at his desk. "Well, one down and only another..." He twiddled his fingers in the air. "Say, twenty or so to go."

"Make your call, Giovanni," I said. "Then it is back to your private cell to cool your heels."

Willie handed Giovanni the phone and in minutes all was plotted and planned. The pilot would go get Jackie. The guards came into the room and Giovanni stood to leave.

# # #

"First, make me a copy of the book," I said, nodding to the book laying on Willie's desk.

He gave me a look and I knew I was stepping beyond what he was willing to share; especially evidence.

"Here's the file," I said. "In date - more or less - sequence of them missing. Starting with Holly..." I laid the pictures on Willie's desk. "A copy of the book in exchange?"

He nodded, stood, took the book to a woman sitting near the wall and gave it to her. She nodded and Willie returned to his desk.

Willie snapped up the pictures of Holly, Myra, and Barbara. "We know these three and they are now free along with the other two from the last parade." He sat down and studied the remaining pictures. "Here's Jackie."

"Off hand," I said. "Do you have any idea who Argus Myles is?"

He shook his head. "Nope." He grinned. "Hey, Preston, you doing anything important?"

"Always," Preston grunted.

"Fine. Find out who Argus Myles is," Willie said and winked at me.

"Where is this guy from?" Preston asked.

"You tell me," Willie replied. "All I have is a name and I know he has money; lots and lots of money." Willie paused. "You might want to check Interpol; he might be international."

"Sure," Preston mumbled.

"Let's check your list from Bingwen against the pictures," Willie said. "Let's eliminate as many as possible... and find them, if at all possible."

CHAPTER TWENTY-FOUR

My Office

Finally, I was in my office, my desk, my space.

I put all my notes on the desk and started to arrange them. When the hairs on the back of my neck start tickling, I know something I think is right, isn't.

What is not right, I thought and stared at the notes.

We had all the critical prospects in jail, yet something didn't gel.

I grabbed a sheet of paper and started my mapping. I put Ping Lin at the top with an arrow going to both Fai Yue and Shaliq Awad. From Fai Yue I connected Zhong and Liang Jin. Above Ping I drew in the buyers connecting them to her.

Shaliq's name was on twice. I squinted at the drawing. *Why*, I thought.

There seemed to be something missing; something I was missing. Everything seemed in place and pat, but yet, my hairs tickled.

I sat there and stared at the names and connecting lines.

What am I missing? I thought.

Shaliq Awad was not a sheik... not a sheik.

Wait a minute! My mind exploded. *If he isn't a sheik, how can he buy at the auction? Where does a guy working in a Chinese buffet kitchen get three hundred thousand dollars?*

Folding up the map, I frowned, grabbed my copy of Ping Lin's book and headed to Chang's.

My question: Did Shaliq Awad ever purchase?

#

I was lucky. Bingwen sat a table sipping his tea. Key word; sipping. A chill coursed down my spine remembering how Willie slurped his tea. I shuddered.

"Nǐhǎo,(hello) Bingwen," I said.

He gazed up at me. "You are early again today, Detective Hargrove." He stood.

"Stay seated," I said and sat down across from him at the table. I slid the stack of copied information across to him. "Go through the names quickly and see if you can find Shaliq Awad."

Bingwen frowned but slid his finger down a column of Chinese characters. He turned the page, all the while shaking his head.

He finally came to end of the list.

"I didn't find Shaliq Awad in the list." He gazed at me. "Why him, if I may ask?"

I shrugged. "I don't know, but something isn't making any sense." I took the copies from Bingwen. "Thanks for help."

Bingwen smiled. "I wasn't much help. Do you want some tea?"

"Maybe later," I said, stood, and headed out of the restaurant.

My mind was in turmoil. Information jumped at me, always coming back to Shaliq Awad.

How does a kitchen worker get invited to an auction? How can he offer an outlandish amount of money... and, Fai Yue plays along?

I strolled back to my office, unlocking the door when it hit.

Where does Shaliq Awad live? Maybe his place can give me a clue.

I relocked the door, pulled my trusty notepad out and checked.

Yes, I do have Shaliq's address. I frowned. I expected the address to be in Lian's area, but instead, it was up in a high-priced residential area. *That doesn't make sense,* I thought.

I headed to my car. *We missed something and I should probably tell Willie, but...*

#

Pulling up to the curb of the high-rise apartment building, I started to question if I was on the right track. I walked into the building and was greeted by security.

"You are here to see?" the guard asked as he stood up from behind the desk.

"Sheik Shaliq Awad."

"I don't believe the sheik is in," the guard said. "Did you have an appointment?"

I nodded.

"I'll call his suite. Your name?"

"Barry Hargrove."

The guard sat and lifted the phone, dialing a number. I watched. Four digits; nine, zero, zero, one. I glanced at the elevator, the dial went from 'B2' to '9' and currently was on level seven.

I realized this was going to take some ingenuity if I wanted to get to his apartment. Obviously, I was going to need to sneak into the lower level parking, but how?

"The sheik is not answering, sir. Would you like to leave a message?"

I shook my head. "I'll get in touch with him later."

Do I call Willie and get a warrant? I thought.

I grinned. *Nope! Let's crash the garage.*

#

Sitting in my car, waiting, watching the garage entrance. Of course, it was keyed.

Timing is everything, Barry, I thought.

Vehicles coming out had to wait for traffic to get out of the driveway. But the vehicles going into the building, the gate had the same amount of time.

Plenty of time for me, I thought. *I just need the right person; and not some little old lady.*

My waiting paid off. A yellow Jaguar convertible driven by a teenager bolted into the driveway. I followed, pulling up behind the

Jaguar. The kid slipped the card in, and the gate opened. Screeching, he sped into the darkness of the building. I followed, slipping through with the gate coming down, almost hitting the back of my car.

Oh, this is going to be fun, I thought, looking at the numbers on each parking spot.

There by the entrance, I saw an empty spot marked 9-1. I decided that had to be Shaliq's parking spot. I drove my car into it. The spot on the opposite side of the large sliding door entrance was marked 9-2. I gazed about, there were only two spots marked with a '9' and I was in one of them. I prayed I was right in my decision.

The teenager approached the big sliding doors and passed his card in front of the reader.

Great! I thought. *So much security.*

The kid disappeared. My chance was gone. I waited.

Soon another car entered the parking area and I watched the young woman get out of her car and head for the doors.

I timed myself, getting out of the car and walking so I would approach the door seconds before her. I pretended to fumble to find my card.

"I have my card out," the woman said. "Here." She passed the card in front of the reader and the door opened.

I'm in, I thought. *Finally.*

We approached the elevator and she, again, slid her card in front of the reader. Stepping in, she cast a glance at me.

"What floor?" she asked.

"Floor? Oh, uh, five," I mumbled, hoping she was on a different floor.

She smiled. "I'm on three." She pressed three then five. "I don't believe I've ever seen you before. New?"

I nodded. "Yesterday."

She shrugged. "I didn't know there was an opening on five." She shook her head. "It is very difficult to get a place in this building. I just love all the security."

"Uh-huh," I mumbled as they elevator doors opened on the third floor.

"Have a lovely day, Mister?" Standing in the elevator doorway, she waited for an answer.

"Mister Reginald Barclay," I offered.

"I'm Evelyn Howard," she said softly. "Perhaps we'll run into each other again."

I nodded, she stepped out, the door closed. I punched nine. The button flashed then was off again.

"Great," I whispered, noticing the custom keyhole beside the button.

The elevator doors opened on floor five. I pushed the 'Close' button and again pushed nine. The doors closed, but nothing. I pushed eight and the elevator started.

CHAPTER TWENTY-FIVE

The Apartment

There has to be an override, I thought and again pushed the nine button, holding it down.

The doors opened on eight and again I pushed the 'Close' button. The elevator doors closed, a bell rang and the elevator continued up.

The elevator doors opened on nine to a luxurious lobby. Skylights above filled the room with light and the lush growth of plants filling the lobby seemed to enjoy it. Two doors greeted me. Each had a number on the door. Remembering the numbers, the guard had punched, I took a chance that the door with a 'One' on it was where I wanted to go.

I stood in front of door one staring at the keypad.

Of course, I thought. *More security. Stupid cards.*

I pulled out my wallet and slipped an old credit card out. Finagling it, I was able to slip it around the door jam and push the door open, having slipped the latch back.

Grinning, I figured the door was designed so when the lock was released, the person only had to push the door open which meant the latch had the curved edge toward the outside rather than the inside.

I was in!

Sheik Shaliq Awad lived in style. This was a penthouse.

I doubted the money he made working in the kitchen even covered the utilities of this place.

Why would somebody who can afford this place work in a Chinese buffet kitchen? My mind wandered as I walked from the lobby to the main room. The hallway from the lobby to the main room was more of a tunnel. The main room soared two floors. The wall of windows overlooked the area, the panoramic vista was breath-taking. A sliding door allowed access to a small balcony. Actually, it was just railing across; there was no actual balcony. I turned and looked back into the room.

Stairs led up to a second story balcony. Beneath the balcony was a large dining room and well-equipped kitchen. I went up the stairs and stood by the wall of the balcony overlooking the living room below. The vista the windows offered was even more fantastic. I could see for miles.

I wandered down the hallway; three doors led to three massive bedrooms, each with its own bath facility.

The largest of the three I guessed was Shaliq's since it had a lived-in look.

What was I looking for?

Nothing stood out. I went to the dresser. A large wooden jewelry case caught my attention.

Jewelry case? A man?

My hand immediately opened the top lid.

A collection of rings scattered across the opening. I picked up the white stone; a diamond. The red was a ruby.

These are not the belongings of a kitchen worker, I thought.

I pulled out the top drawer. Cuff links; gold, silver, jeweled. I pulled open the lower, largest drawer. An assortment of watches greeted me. Again, some gold, silver, jeweled, and leather.

I'm onto something, I thought.

I closed up the jewelry box and glanced at the mirrored doors of the closet. I approached and opened the mirrored doors. It was what I would call another room, but it was a closet filled with clothes: suits, shirts, slacks, ties, and an array of Arabic clothing.

It was then I noticed the rug on the floor. It was facing east.

A prayer rug, I thought.

I stepped back out of the closet, left the bedroom and headed down the hallway for the balcony. Once more, enjoying the breath-taking view, I went down the stairs to the living room. I sat in the over-stuffed chair. I needed to think.

Maybe Shaliq Awad is a real sheik, I thought. *How else could he afford this lifestyle?*

I pulled out my map with everyone's names. I crossed out the two instances of Shaliq's name.

He had to fit in somewhere, I thought

I put his name at the top of the page, above Ping Lin.

It hit!!

Shaliq Awad was the big cheese, not Ping Lin. If Ping Lin was in charge, she would be living in this apartment, not Shaliq. His working in the kitchen was a ruse, something to confuse and confound.

Who would look at a lowly kitchen worker? Plus, he knew about the book. I don't think Fai Yue even knew about it.

"Willie," I whispered. "Are you in for a big shock."

# # #

I walked into 'Missing Persons' office rather proud of myself. Preston noticed me and immediately grabbed a stack of papers, holding them in my direction. I ambled toward him, begrudgingly.

"You and Williamson wanted to know about Argus Myles. He is... was a major trade entrepreneur dealing internationally. He was involved in an air accident last year on December first. It was a private plane accident in Scotland where he resided..." He glanced down at his notes. "Near the Sgurr Fiona pinnacle." He shook his head. "Only seven miles from home. Anyway, there were no survivors with only five aboard the private plane. They were able to identify all but one, a female." He shrugged and made a face showing his disdain, then handed me the papers.

"Thanks, Preston."

I now knew what happened to Gloria. I turned and walked to Willie's desk. "Preston told me about Gloria and Argus Myles." I sat down.

Willie nodded. "Yeah, sorry to hear that."

I grinned.

"What you so happy about?" Willie asked.

"Do you realize Miss Ping Lin is not our big cheese?"

"What do you mean?" Willie stared at me. "Ping Lin isn't the big cheese?"

"Ping Lin was the accountant, if you want to call her that. I bet if you check Shaliq's bank statement, you'll find he pays for the warehouses, the hired help, and whole lot more."

Willie frowned. "Just how did you get privy to all this information?"

"Take a gander at Shaliq's address."

Willie pulled up the information. "So, he lives at... What? I can't even afford that area." He gazed at me. "How?"

"To begin with, I think he might be a real sheik, a minor one, but a sheik. Or, he is making all his money from the auctions, which is a reality considering how much each girl brings at the auction. A couple more auctions and he could go home and have his own kingdom."

"What gave you the insight?" Willie asked.

"I was at my desk and well, the hairs back here..." I reached to the back of my neck. "They kept tickling me. I knew something wasn't right, just didn't know what it was until I saw his address."

Willie gave me that look.

"You checked out his address... with a warrant."

I shrugged. "Maybe."

"Barry! I'm going to slap your butt in jail."

"I'm a detective," I said. "Just doing my job."

"It's called B & E, breaking and entering." He shook his finger at me. "Not allowed."

"Well, I didn't break anything." I hesitated. "You should see the vista view that penthouse has. It's amazing."

"I'll get a warrant." He glared at me. "See? That's how it works. I get a warrant; I go check things out."

I shrugged.

"You are going to have a nice war bonnet with all the feathers this little coup has offered."

Willie leaned back in his chair, locking his fingers together and placing his hands on his chest.

"Yes, life is good and the bad guys are locked up." He sheepishly gazed at me. "Thanks, Barry."

THE END

About the Author

My name is Robert S. Nailor but most people call me Bob.

I'm retired from the federal government. I was a computer geek and still do some programming yet today. One would think I should have plenty of time to write, but I actually seem to have less now. So, to make sure that things work out correctly, I force myself to sit down and write. That doesn't always work. Today, writing is fun and I find it relaxing. I get to visit those fantastic and strange places within my mind and well, if I don't come back right away, there is no longer somebody behind me writing on a pink sheet of paper.

I live with my wife, Violet, in a ranch home snuggled into a small wooded acre in NW Ohio. I was born in Sioux City, Iowa but my parents moved to Ohio in 1953. I have four sons and currently have ten grandchildren - 7 granddaughters and 3 grandsons. Plus, I have 11 great-grandchildren — 5 great-granddaughters and 6 great-grandsons.

My interests are camping (have RV, will travel), gardening, music, cooking and reading. So where do I travel? I've been in 46 of the 50 states and strangely, Hawaii is one of the states I've visited (U.S. Navy) but not Alaska. I have also visited two of our territories - Puerto Rico and the Virgin Islands. Traveling allows me to add the ambiance to my stories and also to some of the characters. Gardening is a bit gamey since we live in the country and have the wildlife visiting us constantly — deer, rabbits, raccoon, birds, squirrels plus many others. So, vegetables don't always make it to harvest, but what does is more than tasty. There are flowers, sometimes too many, to keep me busy. Music? I love New Age music and my favorite group is Mannheim Steamroller... and not just because of their fabulous Christmas albums; I was hooked on them before that. I also have created some of my own electronic music which I've been told is pretty good. Should I mention cooking? I love to cook and do gourmet cooking. Having worked with Boy Scouts for several years, I have taught many boys the basics of cooking beyond hot dogs and beans. I have won quite a few contests. As to what I read; well, obviously a lot of science fiction, fantasy and some Christian. Horror, romance, adventure and other genres are also great reads when they catch my attention with an intriguing tag line or cover.

Bibliography

Novels:

Eternal Blood ~ Book 1 in the Barry Hargrove detective mystery
The Babbling Sphinx ~ Book 2 in the Barry Hargrove detective mystery
The Secret Voice ~ Book 1 in The Amish Singer series
The New York Voice ~ Book 2 in The Amish Singer series
The Amish Voice ~ Book 3 in The Amish Singer series
The Vietnam Voice ~ Book 4 in The Amish Singer series
Pangaea, Eden Lost ~ a Barclay Havens, relic hunter mis-adventure
Three Steps: The Journeys of Ayrold ~ an Irish fantasy for today
2012 Timeline Apocalypse ~ the Mayan calendar comes to an end
At Death's Door ~ a collection of "light" horror stories about death
The Emerald ~ Book 1 in The Shiyula Realm series

Coming Soon...

The Family Voice ~ book 5; can the Amish be forced to move
The Englische Voice ~ book 6; does love really mend all?
The Topaz ~ book 2 in The Shiyula Realm series
Mommy Missing ~ book 4 in the Barry Hargrove mystery series

Anthologies I Am In:

52 Weeks of Writing Tips ~ tips to improve one's writing ability
Telling Tales of Terror ~ essays on how to write horror and dark fiction
Mother Goose Is Dead ~ a collection of favorite fairy tales, fractured
Dead Set: A Zombie Anthology ~ a collection of unusual zombie tales
The Complete Guide to Writing Paranormal-Vol 1 ~ various essays
Nights of Blood 2 ~ different takes on the vampire story
Guide to Writing Science Fiction ~ essays on writing science fiction
Firestorm of Dragons ~ an eclectic collection of dragon stories
Fantasy Writer's Companion ~ essays on writing fantasy
13 Night of Blood ~ 13 amazing vampire tales
Spirits of Blue & Gray ~ a collection of Civil War ghost stories

PLUS more at www.bobnailor.com

This page left blank

Book Four: The Case of Missing Mommy

I sat at my desk, staring at the napkin with all the scribblings connecting the dots of my last case. The door opened, catching me off-guard.

A young boy walked in, marched to my desk, and placed a piggy-bank on it.

"Can you help me?" he asked and crawled onto the chair. "My name is Billy Hopkins, I'm six years old and my mommy is gone."

I smiled at the youngster, noting his blond hair, bright blue eyes, and the blue and red horizontal stripes of his shirt that bulged ever so slightly at the stomach. "Where do you think your mommy is, Billy?" I asked.

He shrugged. "I don't know, but I know you can find her."

I leaned back in my chair. "What makes you so sure?"

"Lian Yoon told me so."

"Lian?"

Billy nodded. "Lian lives next door." He smiled. "He said you're a very good detective and can find my mommy."

Memories of the place where Lian lived sent shivers through my body; and this young boy lived next door to him.

I leaned over my desk, placing my hands together. "Okay. How long has your mother been missing?"

"She worked yesterday and didn't come home." Again, he smiled. "I made a peanut butter jelly sandwich for supper."

"What did you have to eat today?"

"Cereal."

My mind screamed for me to call Child Services, but there was something about Billy's smile. He was innocent. That would be lost with Child Services within a day.

"Are you hungry now? Do you like Chinese food?"

He nodded.

"Let me make a couple of phone calls and then we'll go to Chang's for something to eat. Okay?"

Again, he nodded and pushed the piggy bank toward me. "How much do I owe? Is there enough?"

"For now, nothing," I replied. "Let's see if I can find your mommy."

I picked up the phone and called Lian. He answered on the third ring.

"*Nǐ hǎo* (hello)," Lian said.

"Detective Hargrove, here," I replied. "I have little Billy Hopkins with me. We're going to lunch. Would you join us? My treat. See me at Chang's."

"See you," Lian said and hung up.

I pressed the receiver on the phone and dialed Willie. Two rings and Willie picked up.

"Tell you what, Willie," I started.

"Barry, I don't have time..."

"Listen. I need you to join me for lunch. I have a new client, six-year-old Billy Hopkins. His mommy is missing."

"Chang's?" Willie asked without hesitation.

"See you there," I replied and hung up.

I stood and walked around the desk.

"Okay, Mr. Billy Hopkins. How about we go get something to eat. I have a friend who can help me find your mommy and I also invited Lian to join us."

Billy smiled at me, took my hand, and we walked to the door where I flipped the sign to indicate I was out. We left the office, locking the door when it closed.

#

Intro to book 4; *The Case of Missing Mommy*; current working title, hopefully due out mid/late 2024.